BRIGHTER
Graphite

BRIGHTER

Graphite

Two Novellas by Michael Horvath

Suffern, NY

I would like to thank Stephanie Bart-Horvath, my wife, for the beautiful design of this book and her constant support throughout the long process of finishing this project; my publisher Chris Sulavik, for his enthusiasm and relentless forward momentum; and John Paine, my editor, for the perfect twist.

Brighter Graphite: Two Novellas.

Contact Tatra Press LLC,
292 Spook Rock Road, Suffern, NY 10901.
Library of Congress Control Number: 2008937944

The text was composed by
Stephanie Bart-Horvath.

Book design by Stephanie Bart-Horvath.

ISBN 10: 0-9776142-9-8
ISBN 13: 978-0-9776142-9-5
Distributed by NATIONAL BOOK NETWORK

I dedicate this book to the memory of
my grandmother, Rosa Tall,
whose faith in me was unwavering.

Contents

Graphite..........9

Brighter..........65

Graphite

I regarded my pencil with incredulity.

It was one from a new case that I had arranged, at no small expense, to import from the far south. I was not used to having the graphite core—also referred to (improperly) as the "lead"—snapping off as I scribbled my notes. This was the third of three sharpenings that had done so, a vexing occurrence, as the tedious process of grinding off the wood to spike the beautiful core was consuming more time and concentration than the work at hand. True, I have been accused of applying undue pressure to my writing instruments—a matter, in my view, indicative only of the clarity of my thought and expression (I rarely need to edit), but, admittedly, a factor in my long-standing patronage of the fine products of the Graphite Pencil Works. To call the breakage unusual would hardly state the case; these pencils were famous the world over.

Living up to the high expectations that came with the price, they were far more reliable than the cheap local wares favored by schoolchildren and accountants. The broken cores must be a bizarre anomaly, I thought. I burrowed my hands deep into the cedar-fragrant crate to test two pristine specimens from deep within. Extracting the slender wooden tubes, I loosed a puff of the feather packing, from pest-birds turned in for bounty. The pencils were so impressive I had to stop to admire their balance, color, and texture for a moment before sharpening them to finely honed points. But I was disappointed again. And again. My new case of pencils was spoiled—an expensive and disturbing fact I refused to accept.

I communicated my alarm to several acquaintances who (I thought!) shared my appreciation for quality writing instruments, only to learn, with a shock, that they, too, had the same experience over the previous several years, and had actually changed brands. Chagrined that they had failed to inform me at the time, I sternly took them to task for their negligence. After a great deal of stuttered mollifying, I grudgingly accepted their apologies, but silently vowed to even the score when the time presented itself, as it surely would.

Still smarting from their slight, I contemplated the appalling predicament that faced me. True, I purchased my pencils in vast amounts (at a much better price) and my previous order, consisting of two crates, or twenty-four thousand units, of these most beautiful of mark-making tools had lasted me twelve years. It was profoundly upsetting to realize that those might have been the last of the most perfect pencils ever made—a possibility which instilled a deep sense of regret. But I roused myself. If something could be done, I would see it through, and thus resolved to investigate the mystery in person.

My decision was not spontaneous, or altruistic. It was motivated by pure self-interest, for it was my personal passion, and undeniable intention, to tour the four world capitals of industrial lubricants. Over the years, I had made pilgrimages to Oylee, Siliconia, and Greasemere. I had long been planning a journey to Graphite, the jewel in the friction-free crown of these four great cities. The pleasure of the adventure would be twofold. I had been saving for quite a while, but the timing had not seemed right—until now. The journey could not fail to be enlightening and gratifying, and it certainly could not wait.

Thus committed, I checked the train schedule; I had five short days to put my affairs in order before embarking and applied myself to that end with singular determination.

On Tuesday morning I milled about with others in the pre-dawn dark at the Bilker's Hump station, awaiting the Number Three Express, which would spirit me along the first leg of my journey, to the abominable Mute Warren, an overly large city I detest. If only it lived up to its name! This hub of the rail system held the most extreme noise levels imaginable, from the constant steam whistles signaling train arrivals and departures, to the continual explosive pressures blasted from its factories as they poured and punched out the absurd cast-iron furniture that was all the rage in the finest rooms of Castaphon and Pallid's Pike. This round-the-clock cacophony forced its rude inhabitants to speak with exaggerated volume, never noticeably modified, even in those rare moments of quiet. The factory emissions and the metal smelting fouled the air, rendering any time spent there an unendurable eternity. The schedule called for only a short hiatus in Mute Warren and I fervently hoped it would hold.

As the venerable Number Three chugged into the station, trailing great billows of steam and a settling cloud of carbon soot belched from its iron belly, I thrilled: My journey was beginning. Such a powerful sight could only herald success. First in line, I boarded and headed directly to my reserved berth.

The compartment looked comfortable enough. I settled in, arranging my belongings in a fashion that would afford maximum convenience and efficiency. My travels had convinced me a private berth was worth the cost, as it minimized undue annoyance—I had little patience for most people any time, but in the morning I had tolerance for none. The train jerked, then slowly moved out of the station, and I checked my watch—5:15 a.m., right on time.

Pleased with the punctual departure, I sat back, watching the dark landscape zip by as the train gained speed. The geometric urbanity of the city gave way to the casual arrangements of the suburbs, then those thinned to the cool green of the countryside as the sky grew pink. The sun was starting to peak over the twin foothills (dubbed Bilker's Rump by the local wags) that marked the southernmost claim of the city. It was a beautiful scene, suffused with roseate light, which also implied the advent of rain. I basked in the glorious scenery until another clock—my stomach—informed me I had neglected my morning meal. I roused myself and headed off to breakfast.

Being the lone diner in the car, I received the full attentions of the decrepit attendant. I slowly (and repeatedly) placed my order and read the papers—yes, papers in the plural—until my food arrived. Due to the man's lack of speed, the unsatisfying repast was delivered lukewarm to my table, but I did not have the heart (or stomach) to send it back to the kitchen, lest I starve. The ancient waiter toddled off without a word of apology to my sharp rebukes, pushing his little cart, without which he no doubt would have toppled over. The jellied mangoes were too sweet, with none of the tartness one would reasonably expect. I regarded the oatmeal with distaste; it resembled a bowl of lumpy and discolored plaster.

Deciding not to chance this horrid breakfast stew, I instead poured a single dollop of milk into my coffee, which sank from sight without discernibly lightening the beverage. A tentative sip revealed it must have been brewed at least two days prior to being served; it was bitter as gall. I shook my head, lamenting the sorry state of gourmandise. My appetite thus slaked, I paid my bill (sans gratuity), returning to my compartment to while away the hours and my hunger.

The sun was well up now, burning off the morning mists from the nooks and creases in the hillsides. The green of spring and the sharp blue sky induced me to open the compartment window and take several deep breaths of the bracing air, but I soon was compelled to close it, the oxygen-rich atmosphere making me heady. It was a pleasant day and I resolved to enjoy my journey.

My mind strayed to several subjects of recent preoccupation; I reached for my notebook to jot down a few more thoughts concerning the dormant ambition of the inert. While hastily detailing new insights into that old chestnut involving the behavior of bubbles in a vacuum, my pen malfunctioned. In a lurid gush it expended its reservoir of ink onto the page and thence, by virtue of gravity, onto my pants. My reaction to impede the effects of the accident completed the horrible fiasco; my hand jerked across the page and negated, in a wash of ink, what may well have been significant conclusions. I dropped my notebook and stood in a rage, helplessly watching as the inky shadow spread down the left leg of my fine hand-woven miniature tartan plaid pants. I had no doubt they were ruined but, being the match to the jacket and vest I sported, I slipped my braces and struggled out of them. I inserted one of my monogrammed handkerchiefs into the left leg to stay the ink from transferring to the facing fabric. Hurriedly, I donned the tailored black wool riders I pulled from my rucksack, then hailed a porter. I explained the situation in a frantic rush.

The porter—Bebo, by name—was not reassuring, and explained that the cleaner had taken another position and had not been replaced. But he would see what he could do and left with my spoiled trousers. Despite my recent resolution to enjoy the journey, my mood had turned glum. The trip was not proceeding well at all. And the mishap with the pen made me pine for the simplicity of a well-made pencil. To top things off, we would arrive in Mute Warren in less than three hours.

Desultory and groggy from waking early to make the train, I decided to nap through the trial of lunch. I would need my strength at the transfer point, God knows, and would find a quick bite there to help pass the time in that purgatory. Though we were chugging through the Vulvine Gorge, I fell asleep, having seen the damp and uneasy wonder several times.

A timid tapping on compartment door gently brought me round, and after a moment's confusion I came to, refreshed and cognizant. It was the porter Bebo, to whom I had entrusted my tartans. He signaled me with a little smile and a slight wave. Perhaps it was his good-natured personality, or maybe a premonition, but I felt optimistic despite the damage I had endowed upon my trousers. I opened the door, bidding the small fellow to enter.

In a rush, he explained that this was my lucky day, for as he explained the impossible cleaning task to his fellow porters, he had been overheard by one of the passengers, who demanded to examine the damage. The passenger grandiosely declared that he would need a private berth and a quart of the finest bourbon to be had from the club car. The swell had further instructed Bebo to bill the owner of the pants for all costs incurred. Bebo complied with trepidation, relinquishing my tartans to this imperious man and ushering him into an unused compartment, where the stranger gave one last order, that being a small collapsible table, which was soon delivered, along with the top-shelf whiskey. Bebo was to return in an hour, at which time, he was assured, the damage would be completely reversed. Efficient Bebo reported that this man had laid out a number of bottles and tubes in preparation for his task, then opened the bourbon and poured himself three stiff fingers. Saluting the porter formally, he drank off the potent draught with nary a shiver before shooing the train attendant out.

When Bebo returned, the man was well into the bottle, good-natured but incoherent. He motioned at Bebo to take the trousers and go, which he hurriedly did, sensing a potentially uneasy situation.

Bebo thus proffered the pants for my scrutiny. To my eye, it was as if the damage was never inflicted; the disaster was undone, my tartans miraculously restored to their pristine state. Overjoyed, I slapped Bebo on the back, in congratulation, before regaining my composure.

"Ah, they are beautiful. But, Bebo," I queried, "what is this oddly pleasant smell that imbues my pants?"

Bebo explained that he had learned from the other porters that the gentleman who had saved my trousers was a painter of some repute. He had not actually removed the stain from the fabric, but fixed it with solutions, and then perfectly matched the pattern with oil colors, accounting for the smell and heavy stiffness with which the once sinuous material was now invested. The workmanship was superb, of the highest quality. I thanked Bebo heartily and tipped him well (though not as well as if my pants were not still ruined), and settled the painter's exorbitant bar tab before sending the porter on his way. I tested the surface of the repair and my finger came away clean. The clever artist must have used a drying agent in his pigments, which rendered the material stiff and unyielding. I worried about the craquelure that surely would eventually ensue, but my concern proved unfounded.

While I was folding the tartans into my rucksack, I heard another soft knock at the door. It was Bebo again.

"Excuse me much, sir," he stammered, "but the gentleman has just finished with this." He displayed my monogrammed handkerchief with which I had tried to stanch the flow of ink. Instead of the immaculate white with gold monogram, the field was black. The gold letters stood out in a bold impasto. Attached was a barely legible note in pencil, thanking me for my hospitality (the drinks, I supposed) and presumably signed, though I could not make out a pronunciation from whatever letters I fancied were written there.

Bebo bowed gracefully, announcing that we would arrive at Mute Warren station in ten minutes.

I have never since had occasion to wear my tartans, nor can I imagine a situation in which I would. I have had them framed, and exhibit them in the foyer, along with my monogrammed handkerchief and the illegible note. Though I do not know his name, or anything of his career, I will venture that, for a painter, he made a fine tailor.

Pulling into the station, I felt the clamor before actually hearing it. I fetched from a pocket of my rucksack the wax-covered pignoli nuts so skillfully wrought by the miniaturist artisans of Rawwoody, and fit them into my ears to block the excessive volume of that forsaken city. Thus steeled, I exited the train, wading into the abominable cacophony of Mute Warren.

Despite the sound blockers, I soon developed a splitting headache—another burden to bear, along with my baggage. A query to a member of the local constabulary revealed, in loud declamation, that I could do no wrong in lunching at a cafe several blocks west, toward the ugly center of town.

This safe harbor proved to be anything but that. The rude patrons of the greasy eatery gawked with menacing curiosity as I entered, puffing heavily. Satisfied I was harmless to their sordid plots, they resumed their loud and stupid conversations. I would have left was I not so weary, and I had seen no other restaurants on the way. I settled inconspicuously at a corner table, far from the light and glazed eyes of the cafe regulars, composing myself as best I could, awaiting service.

Presently, a vastly obese waiter wearing a filthy apron and skimpy shirt emerged from the murk to silently stare at me, pen and pad poised for my order. Apparently, there was no menu. Rather than futilely recite a litany of my culinary desires, I thought quickly and ordered the house specialty. What that might be, I had no idea, but it was certain to be already prepared, and I had no desire to spend more time here than was absolutely necessary.

I had just finished reading a featured article on the miraculous aspects of utopian metals when the gargantuan waiter lumbered toward me, holding a plate, his huge exposed belly swinging with every step. He said something as he served, but, due to my sound blockers, I missed what it was. I hastily removed the waxed nuts (so thoughtfully provided with tiny handles) but, by that time, the broad back of the man was melding once again with the gloom.

The heaped plate was steaming, and I was so famished that I confess my mouth was watering. I cautiously prodded the "special," inspecting it and attempting to identify the ingredients, with great difficulty. It appeared to be a minced meat of some sort, served over a glutinous vegetable (probably okra) poised atop a noodle-like mass which adhered aggressively to my fork. The smell was not unpleasant, however, and a tentative mouthful assured me the stuff was, indeed, edible, if uncommonly bland. I set to, eating the bulk of it without further thought, interrupted only once by my waiter, who brought a tumbler of water and a gravy boat containing an anonymous congealed sauce, which, I supposed, was to be liberally applied to the "special." At that I demurred, putting it aside so I would not have to look at it. There was no salt or pepper at the table; the locals must have considered the concoctions of this place spicy enough for their pedestrian tastes. Without much thought, I suffered down the rest of the food, reflecting instead on the fascinating article I had read. In that, at least, was food for thought, as well as much that could be incorporated into my own research on the exaltation of the inanimate.

It was a dark day indeed for penmanship; the bill was a baffling cypher, and I puzzled over it as the waiter stood by impassively. Uncertain of the amount, I handed over a large bill, which surely would cover the lackluster fare. I waited for my change, but the fool did not return, and steadfastly ignored my attempts to catch his eye. Wisely deciding not to press the issue, I even left a small gratuity, making this the third most expensive meal I had ever eaten.

By now the sky had clouded over. It was dreadfully hot and humid as I tramped back toward the station.

Garbage reclamation plants vented their stinking methane emissions and iron factories pumped out filth, which blackened entire neighborhoods. The city's raucous din pressed even through my noise blockers. It started to rain but I was glad; perhaps it would dampen the noise and rinse clean the defiled air.

The squalor of Mute Warren is remarkable only in its profusion. Every social situation that I witnessed while waiting bore the unmistakeable stamp of the place. The bellowing speech and uncouth laughter that defined the city were amplified by the architecture of the station, creating a racket to drive poor visitors mad.

Salting my wounded psyche was the sudden appearance of a group of buskers, who made an entrance like a troupe of baboons scouting new territory. They proceeded to entertain the waiting horde with displays of juggling, acrobatics, and cheap magic tricks. The mime's pathetic attempts at gestural humor filled me with a silent rage. I wished the most horrible of futures on him and his.

Relieved at the sight of my train, I took a place in line as the passengers queued up in the drizzle. The porter shouted in my ear the entire time and his excessive volume practically blew away the meaning of his words. It appeared that there had been a ticketing error; reserved seats and private compartments would not be honored, unfortunately. He yelled that he was sorry for the inconvenience and, if anyone so desired, their reservations would be upheld on the next southbound train, due to arrive in seven hours. Desperate to leave the damnable place, I decided to take a chance, hoping to not be paired with a prattling idiot for the next four hours.

My advantageous position in line served me well; I quickly claimed the lone available window seat, located, unfortunately, directly across from the water closet. I refuse to relate the most revolting series of humiliations to which anyone has ever been subjected, for it would require disturbing memories that were difficult to repress. I will say, however, that the perpetrator of these outrages was a waste of human flesh. If only nose blockers were sold on the train! I would have paid a high price indeed to purchase a pair, but foolishly passed on the chance during my last visit to Rawwoody, seeing little application and thinking them frivolous.

My crisis ended when the train pulled into the station at Punity. A few haggard souls boarded to replace the wretched group that departed, both sets undoubtedly visiting incarcerated relatives. Punity's singular industry is the confinement and care of the most reprehensible criminals of the region. I have always thought it peculiar, but touchingly civilized, that the condemned were allowed their choice of execution: by noose, garrotte, immolation, flagellation, immurement, quartering, impalement, poison, etc. Last requests that truly lasted.

En route once again, we headed into bad weather. Fresh air from cracked windows quickly replaced the sour by-product of my former companion. There was now ample room, the car being only half full, so I was not bothered with a another seatmate. Finally relaxing, I mentally composed a letter to Provincial Railpath, the company that ran the line, detailing the outrageous inconvenience I was forced to endure because of *their* ticketing error while in *their* care.

That task completed, I checked the time. The train was scheduled to arrive in Graphite just before 9:00 p.m. I decided to dine onboard, though at the moment I was not hungry, my lunch "special" proving to have impressive staying power.

I had acquired a thick guidebook for the town and its

outlying districts, to best utilize the time allotted for my visit. In the crush of my departure, I had merely skimmed the tome, but I now paged through the book avidly. The guide—ten years out of date—contained detailed information about many attractions that were of keen interest to me. The Graphite Museum was an obvious must-do and I could hardly wait to visit the factories. Both the pencil works and the lubricant mills had daily tours. The graphite mines—the lifeblood of this burgeoning industrial town—had restricted access, though an acquaintance claimed a well-placed pittance would open doors for the determined pilgrim. And, certainly, a dip in Graphite Lake was essential to a serious tourist like myself. I was anxious to partake in the rich life the town offered. I was reading about the curious customs of the region when it was announced that seating for dinner was to begin. Reluctantly, I closed the book.

The evening meal was simple but excellent, and started with a delicious suet soup which was richer than the northern versions, the cracklings being especially satisfying. My main course, a baked eel pie with apples and garlic, was a trifle overdone. A bitter herb salad, accented with capers, rounded things out, all served by an eager and polite waiter. Imbibing a thimble of port after supping, I returned to my seat.

We had passed through the storm; the setting sun cast a glorious rainbow through the sprinkles. The wilderness was aglow in the orange light of the sunset, but the day soon drew to a close.

Though due to arrive at my destination in only forty minutes, the wait was interminable. At last the train slowed as it rounded a bend. The window—a black rectangle—gave no idea of the lay of the town. The train whistled, alerting residents that visitors would soon be sharing their hospitality. As it squealed to a stop, a final blast of steam announced our arrival. Aquiver with excitement, I collected my belongings and joined the jostling line of those exiting. Stepping off the train, a thrill ran up my spine as I planted my foot on the station platform, which caused a puff of finely pulverized graphite around the edge of my shoe and revealed a fine mold of the pattern on the sole as I stepped away. The place was pure magic! Ah, Graphite, at long last!

The breeze was clean, cool, and invigorating. I took a deep breath and slowly exhaled, enjoying the contentment of fulfilling a lifelong ambition well ahead of schedule.

Graphite Lodge, the porter informed me, was a twenty-minute walk due east; I could hardly miss it. I passed rows of shops and blocks of quaint cottages, none of which were alight: Graphite retired early. I encountered few late stragglers on the damp street, but each nodded or smiled as they bustled past. So polite and such good habits—I was already thoroughly charmed by the place.

The lodge loomed before me suddenly. It was set back from the street, and a single huge light illuminated the sign hung from the columned porch. Its sheer size brought me up short, despite my having read its description in the guidebook. It is the single most impressive building in the town, a lovely neoclassical structure that sacrificed human scale. Displacing an entire city block and containing 327 rooms, it employs 14 percent of the town's population.

I trekked across the expanse of patterned rug to check in with the courteous clerk, declining the bellboy's offer to help. Climbing to the fourth floor, I found my room at the extreme end of the corridor. Panting,

I let myself in; a quick glance revealed my room to be small, clean, and sufficient. Though I had been sitting most of the day, exhaustion overtook me. Like the rest of the town, I retired early.

A rap on the door and a cheery "Eight o'clock, sir!" roused me from slumber. I jumped from bed, refreshed, and tended to my ablutions, carefully trimming my mustache to put on my best face for the town and its people.

Lightly breakfasting on coffee and kale muffins, I consulted the guidebook map and set out to explore Graphite.

The sky was cloudless, the sun bright—but what strange light it cast! Brittle and metallic, throwing weak shadows, it reminded me of the lumination that occurs during a solar eclipse. I did not take long to unravel the mystery; it was due to the profusion of graphite particles adrift in the balmy air, a notable delight of the town. Unable to suppress a smile, I stepped off the dusty porch and onto the gray-powdered path to the street, causing leaden puffs with every footfall. I was utterly bewitched.

Strolling north, I studied the old and quirky architecture, mostly houses. The thin layer of powder veiling them effected a certain cohesion, a refreshing sameness that marshaled the different styles and hues into a muted symphony of gray.

I went slowly, not missing a thing. Men leaving for their shift at the mills happily whistled to themselves or clustered in good-natured groups. Children—their togs and skin already burnished a lovely shade of gray—frisked about in gritty yards like adorable pewter trophies, enveloped in graphite auras stirred by rowdy play; scolding mothers hung early washes to dry in the warm metallic sunshine.

Such sights overwhelmed me and tears welled in my eyes. It was profoundly gratifying to witness the harmony between the inert and the animate, in a balance so perfect that I never imagined it possible. And yet here it was: the flawless model, the ideal reality.

The museum can be found on the corner of Schist Street and Carbondale Lane. Arriving early, I tarried in the nearby stores, which were open and doing a lively business. I visited several shops before finding souvenirs that fit both my taste and the needs of the intended recipients.

For myself, I purchased a new worry stone of high-quality graphite, with its greasy feel comforting between the thumb and forefinger. Exploring a secondhand shop, I stumbled across a massive bronze antique pencil pointer, a true trophy piece, which I snapped up without haggling over the price. The blade was still sharp, if a little rusty; I doubt that it was ever used.

For my nieces, I purchased a gross of #2 graphite drawing bars—enough to color their mother's house a fine dark shade of gray, I daresay—a gift for which I would surely suffer at the hands of my sister, thoughtful as it was. For my nephew, John, I purchased a large (and expensive) tube of the highest-rated graphite powder, enough to satisfy his lubrication needs for years to come. Tempted to buy similarly impressive gifts for my "friends," I realized my true motive was to induce jealousy, and was thus antithetical to the nature of gift-giving, and so resisted the impulse.

A row of penny machines caught my eye and closer scrutiny revealed great bargains to be had for a pittance. I thought to augment the children's gifts with cunning graphite trinkets but the blasted machines were jammed, all twelve of them. While there was no evidence of criminal intent, I felt cheated of my twelve cents. Annoyed, I moved on, as it was getting late.

While I was dawdling in the shops, the museum had opened some time before. I hurried up the grand gray-dusted stairs to the top, where a sleepy boy lazily pushed the settling grit with a broom, moving the heavy powder from one ill-defined point to another, his wake an obscure dance chart of half-hearted effort.

The museum is a virtual treasury of the glorious history and lore of this noble mineral. Permanent exhibits clearly detailed, with fine examples, every facet of carbon formation—represented, in its natural state, only by diamonds and graphite. Most of the placards had a touch of lyricism to the texts, but such a fascinating subject naturally lends itself to poetry. Highlights included a twelve-ton graphite boulder, which was mined locally, and a room entirely composed of graphite inlay, the furniture as well as the walls, creating a darkly wondrous receiving room suitable for an emperor. I purchased a plethora of postcards of this Eighth Wonder, the work of a town artisan, whose obsession far surpassed my own. A gallery of diamonds, both in natural state and cut, exemplified the extreme range of naturally occurring carbon: diamonds, the hardest material in nature, claiming an unassailed 10 on the tensile scale, though I reserve the soft spot in my heart for graphite, which rates a modest 2.2.

A temporary exhibition of pencil sketches of town scenery drawn by children from the local orphanage completed my tour of the galleries. The imagination of the young mind is astonishing; Graphite would not lack for future artists!

To families journeying to Graphite, I urge a visit to this enlightening institution, as there is much to marvel at and learn. Young children, especially, will be entranced at the breathtaking range of possibilities that the museum provides.

Enthralled by the exhibits, I had toured right through the lunch hour. In the museum snacking bar, I nibbled on braised goose livers and roasted kale (which I learned was the local cash crop, explaining its attendance at every meal). I cannot, in all honesty, recommend the food there.

I did not emerge into the light of the day again until 4:00 p.m. The same lad was sweeping the same step, keeping the burgeoning graphite at bay. I descended to the walk, exhausted but exhilarated, since great museums have an energy-sapping quality. Dedicated to a single theme, the Graphite Museum reveals the vast applications of its subject with dramatic power.

I took a circuitous route back to the lodge. The day shift was ending; the hale and hearty factory workers, coated a shiny gray from their day's labors, made their way home. Some dodged into the Graphite Grille for a comradely drink before pursuing their ultimate destination. I did so as well.

The bar was two-deep with loud men waving money. Friendly slaps to their fellows' backs set off explosions of graphite dust from their overalls. These were men who liked to take their work home with them, I thought, chortling over that nugget till the waitress came with my order, a pint of Grismeister, the local lager. With the first sip of the robust beverage I relaxed, enjoying the camaraderie of the patrons.

Upon my return to the lodge, I thoroughly washed; gouts of gray water spun down the drain. Hopefully, there were special traps in the plumbing to filter out the cherished material. Despite vigorous effort, my skin retained a certain gray cast, which added character to my otherwise bland complexion. I donned a clean white shirt for dinner and thought to find a laundry the next day.

The cavernous dining room was nearly empty—a benefit of traveling off-season. Due to the powerful attractions of the town, I knew, the place would be crammed with tourists during the season.

An interesting article in the *Graphite Gazette* noted that the life expectancy in the area was seven years longer than the Provincial average. A local physician opined that perhaps the waters of Graphite Lake were truly curative, and suggested a methodical scientific inquiry be undertaken.

Awaiting dessert, I mentally planned the next day's agenda. After enjoying the delicious kale custard, I retired. Falling into a deep sleep, I was visited by many pleasant dreams, all of them coated in delightful shades of gray.

I awoke charged with an energy I had not felt in years. Kale croissants and coffee were my breakfast. I repaired to my room and gathered my soiled garments, anxious to get under way. I solicited the desk clerk about a responsible laundry. He laughed, assuring me I would have no trouble finding one. The laundries comprised the third largest industry in Graphite, trailing only the factories and the lodge itself. With directions to the laundry district, I set off.

The early risers were already starting their day. The sweeping of pulverized graphite from walks seemed to top the to-do lists. A mother made a game of pounding the stuff from hung carpets, her children gleefully squealing in the glistening fog created.

I strolled through the better part of town, where impressive mansions housed the graphite barons and the directors of the industries. Teams of gardeners washed down the expansive lawns with high-pressure hoses. I stopped to admire an impressive bed of lilies, which the gardeners had not yet tended. The blossoms looked as if sculpted from delicate gunmetal, serviced by pewter-winged butterflies.

The laundry district sprawled for roughly four square blocks of washhouses and related suppliers. After several unsatisfactory interviews with proprietors, I chose White's Wash, based solely on my impression of Mr. White. Conservative, polite, and well groomed, Mr. White assured me my laundry would be delivered by 6:00 a.m. From the relatively clean condition of my clothing, he deduced I was a visitor and asked if I had yet visited the museum. I enthusiastically informed him I had, first thing, and praised the remarkable collection. Mr. White nodded and smiled with satisfaction. Tipping my hat, I left in high spirits.

An inattentive worker, trundling an enormous bin of fresh-washed linens, cursed as a wheel sank into a depression hidden by the pervasive blanket of graphite dust, upsetting the cart and spoiling the wet load of whites. I chuckled at his plight: such are the pitfalls of Graphite!

The factories—low-slung brick buildings of a similar age, neatly arranged to allow for potential expansions—were visible in the distance. Fifty-meter-high exhaust chimneys vented a heavy haze of fine graphite powder twenty-four hours a day. Since the fall was heavier here than on the other side of town, I opened my umbrella.

Having decided last night to satisfy the reason for my journey, I intended to visit the pencil works straightaway. I wanted my doubts laid to rest, to be assured that I was simply the unlucky recipient of a shipment that had been damaged in transit or by an overlooked mishap in the woodworking division—nothing more. Applying a firm finger to the buzzer at the door marked "Visitors," I waited, trembling with anticipation.

The door opened and a well-scrubbed young woman with ruddy cheeks shyly beckoned me in. Asking my name (I had written in advance), she excused herself, moving to a desk to make a note, in pencil, on a list. Her cheeks flared a deeper red, as if she was in a state of perpetual embarrassment, a comely trait. She ushered me through another door and excused herself, explaining that the tour manager would join me for an excursion through the plant.

The manager soon arrived, effusing corporate goodwill, introducing himself as Fennery Palastoma. Aware of my letter seeking an explanation for the brittle cores, he said he would be pleased to answer any questions during our walk-through.

"It is heartening that some people still take an active interest in the production of fine writing leads," he said with false cheer. "Attendance for the tours has dropped off steadily for some time now. We are considering the tours to be discontinued altogether. But, as a loyal and long-term client, we take your concern seriously. I can assure you that all is in order here. Every pencil manufactured is produced exactly as the very first one. You will see so for yourself."

"Leads"? I was outraged, put on my guard. No true pencil man would refer to the graphite cores as "leads." "Inserts," perhaps, but never "leads." He suggested we start the tour.

"Yes, indeed. Please. Show me," I challenged. The proof of the pudding is in its making. I was in no mood for official corporate mealy-mouthing.

Palastoma picked up on my hostility. "My good sir," he soothed, "as a man who prizes quality, I appreciate what you perceive as a distressing situation. But let me assure you that our graphite product is as fine and true as ever. I suspect your misfortunes with our pencils had nothing whatsoever to do with their manufacture. The broken leads most likely transpired in shipping. Even with recent advances in transportation and packing, it occurs more than I like to admit. The high standards that have distinguished our pencils for two hundred years are still vigorously practiced to this day. The graphite that we use is naturally pure—I personally guarantee that. We use the same materials as we always have: the incense cedar, the same clay, of local origin, and the graphite, which, I am sure you are aware, is the purest mined in the entire world. And," he added, "not to *labor* the point, but our workforce is the most skilled in the industry. Hand-picked apprentices work four years side by side with masters before being granted journeyman status."

Palastoma offered a smug smile after bleating out the company's position on my complaint. An icy stare was my only comment. Uncomfortable, the company lackey cleared his throat. "Let's start the tour then, shall we?"

First, the receiving department, where the raw materials for pencil production were delivered: pulverized graphite from the mills, clay from the lake beds, incense cedar logs harvested from magnificent, fragrant groves in the Dolmens. We spent an hour in the mixing room, where graphite powder and clay were combined in "secret proportion" to produce the "perfect material" from which the "long-lasting" cores were rolled.

In the carpentry shop, craftsman rough-cut the incense cedar logs into planks, refining them, after a number of logical steps, into "slats," which were then scored, and the writing cores laid into the grooves. An identical slat was glued to the first; sawed into pencil lengths, the units were sanded into the familiar hexagonal shape.

Next was the eraser department. The first order of business was the ferule cut for the metal sleeve. The rubber eraser tip was inserted into the sleeve, then clamped into place. Mr. Palastoma told me, in a whisper, that the company was looking into nondrying rubber tips. "Because," he sniffed, "a dry eraser is as useful as a bookmark at a convention of illiterates." As if the rest of the industry had not been trying to solve this same problem for years!

Every step in the manufacture was performed with economy and efficiency. I was impressed by the advanced machinery, the factory's workers, and the management (my tour guide being an exception, but even he did his job as company tout well). The tour itself was academic. I had known every step of pencil production, forward and backward, by the time I was nine, which aided my scrutiny of the processes involved in the factory. All was well; I could detect no shortcuts, no missteps, or errors in production. And yet a tickle of doubt nagged at me as the pompous Palastoma selected a fresh pencil from the assembly line, savoring it under his nose as he would a fine cigar.

"Aaaah!" he said. "For you sir, with our compliments!" With a flourish he tucked it into the breast pocket of my black herringbone slack-jacket.

Thanking him in a formal tone, I shook his hand as he wished me a wonderful visit and an easy trip home. Our hands disengaged, as did we; Palastoma to his office, and I to the graphite mills.

Distracted, I found the tour there of limited interest; it consisted primarily of huge rollers grinding the newly mined graphite schist into increasingly minute particles, depending on its intended application. The air was thick with graphite particulate, the ancient venting machinery inadequate to its task. The noise was tremendous. Not having the foresight to bring my sound blockers, I soon developed a headache and cut my visit short, thinking to return later to finish the tour.

I arrived at the lodge exhausted and spent the rest of the day relaxing to ease my throbbing head. The curried kale dinner helped somewhat and by eight o'clock I was feeling better. As distasteful as the task was, I thought I should write a note of thanks to Mr. Palastoma.

My skepticism was inflamed, however, like a carbuncle that needed lancing. Thus, I pointed the pencil he had presented to me, in my antique sharpener, nearly swooning at the intoxicating fragrance released in the cedar shavings. I placed the point to the delicate surface of the foolscap. It snapped at the first stroke, and I broke with it, sobbing at the loss—not merely my own, but civilization's as well.

Sleep that night was dreadful, marked by vesper sweats and deranged dreams. I woke out of sorts, with a dyspeptic stomach. The day reflected my melancholy mood—a gloomy grisaille tableau, still and menacing. I pulled the shade. A dip in the lake was called for; perhaps its tonic waters would relieve my ailments and somber mood.

The desk clerk cautioned me against my plans—rain was expected. I coolly acknowledged his warning and he reluctantly supplied the quickest route to my destination, which lies south of town, near the ancient cemetery and the clay pits.

The mantle of air was humid and heavy, without a breeze. The walk was long, but gave me a chance to stretch my aching muscles and clear my cluttered head. A dark line on the gray horizon drew my attention and quickened my pace.

The road narrowed to little more than a soft path of graphite cutting through the gray-green growth. Glimpsing the lake while rounding a rise, I descended to the hollow that cupped it.

It was an extraordinary sight. The lake nestled in a wide beach of magnificent graphite dunes, some more than seven feet high. The water, glassy and flat, mirrored the leaden sky. I walked out on a ferry slip and peered across the widest stretch of the water. The ferry was moored to the slip on the far side; a strange accommodation, as one could easily traverse the lake on foot in forty-five minutes. But no ferryman was present and I was quite alone.

Above the dunes, where the green started, I passed a large cottage of exquisite character but long abandoned. I peeked through one of the broken windows; surely, it once served as the summer residence of a graphite baron, retaining much of its original grandeur despite its long disuse.

I disrobed for my dip as the wind whipped up, blowing tendrils and veils of gray powder from the peaks of the dunes. I enjoyed the greasy feel of the graphite under my feet and made my way to the water, which now swelled and rolled with the wind. The water was surprisingly warm and I waded out till only my neck and head were above the water, noting that the surface was coated with floating graphite powder that deposited on me with every wave that broke against my body. I fancied I was bathing in liquid lead, sans the heat. My swimming suit and I were soon the same color of all that surrounded me; I was being baptized in a truly elemental style.

The lake was not deep. I was midway across, the water no higher than my chest, when it occurred to me that the lake might be an abandoned mining pit, perhaps one of the first sites exploited by the itinerant graphite miners who founded the town centuries ago.

Diving under the water, I immersed myself in the silvery-gray liquid. Breaking the surface, I felt the first evidence of rain. Heavy drops dimpled the rippling surface of the lake. I turned shoreward: The drops were setting off thousands of minute gray explosions as they impacted on the dunes and beach. Leery of being caught in a lake saturated with an electrically conductive element, I made for the shore, though I had yet to see or hear any evidence of lightning. A voice from behind startled me, stopping me dead in my tracks.

"Hallo there! Mind your aft!"

Shocked, I turned to behold the small, battered ferry poled along by a wizened old man.

"Get aboard, man! Ah, you don't want to be muckin' about out here in this weather—now give me your hand before you're fried to a crisp!" He was yelling into the blustering wind, which was churning up large, heavy waves that made my progress difficult.

I gripped the proffered hand of the boatman. With surprising strength and skill, the gnarly little man pulled me from the water and into the ferry, hardly upsetting the boat.

"No, you can't swim here in this weather, oh no! Didn't they tell you where you been staying?"

He shook his head in consternation when I shrugged, then turned to inspect the storm bearing down on us from behind. The sky darkened dramatically; flashing bolts of lightning erupted from the blanketing clouds with ear-splitting cracks and deep muffled rumbles of thunder. The wind gusted, blowing the stinging rain sideways, and churning up heavy swells that swamped the boat. I held on tight.

"She's a-coming!" The ferry man bellowed gleefully. "Here!"

He thrust the other pole at me, and I pitched in. With difficulty, we made the ferry slip through the driving rain. The codger leaped off the ferry and expertly secured his boat, then helped me to the shore.

"Grab your gear," he shouted. I ran across the beach, my feet clotting with great clumps of wet graphite. The going was difficult, the footing treacherous.

"Come on!" he ordered, motioning impatiently. I

gathered my soaked clothes into a big wet ball and stumbled after the ferryman.

A blinding flash in the lake and the ear-splitting peal that followed thrilled me along to the sailor's side. We scuttled up the slippery slope of graphite basin in silence, save for grunts and groans of exertion. Gray rivulets sluiced down the hillside, carrying more graphite down to the shore.

Through the hard rain I saw a small cabin near the entrance to the cemetery. The ferryman blundered ahead, slipping in the mud, then carefully wiped his feet before entering the hovel. I followed suit, but less fastidiously, eager to be out of the downpour. The cabin, however, was not totally dry; the boatman entered a puddle in the middle of its single room, staring at the roof, from which issued a steady stream of water. Grousing under his breath, he rattled through a cupboard, returning with a battered pot, which he placed under the leak.

"Damn hole. Damn water . . ." he muttered to himself, suddenly turning to me. "Damn swimming, hey?"

I smiled weakly. The boatman shambled away to dig through a battered chest, returning with a pair of clean but threadbare towels, and handed one to me. Though meager as cheesecloth, I draped it over my shoulders.

Then he screwed up his face in a grimace of humor. "At one time, they're talking resorts out here! Imagine that? Welcome to lightning lake!" The little man silently shook at his joke.

"Well, I'm much obliged, sir, for the helping hand," I told him, smiling politely. "I would still be muddling around out there if not for you."

"Not muddling," he replied seriously. "You'd be boiled alive. Like a lobster."

I extended my hand and introduced myself. With a firm grip he took my hand and gave it one decisive shake. "Captain Edmund Parch. Retired," he said. "Just call me Parch."

He made a vague gesture. "Have a sit down . . . in the chair."

The old seaman claimed the favored seat; the only other chair looked, and was, uncomfortable. From the table between us, he picked up one of a number of small metal discs and inspected it critically, snorting and humming as he turned it round and round. Pulling a small file from one of his many shirt pockets, he set to work on the edges, smoothing irregularities, squinting at his progress. This went on for some time; he seemed to have forgotten my presence, which I found awkward.

"You do quality work, Parch," I said, breaking the silence.

"Hah?" He jumped at the sound of my voice. "Well, . . ." He avoided my eyes, embarrassed by his forgetfulness.

"What are you making?" I inquired, to put him at ease.

"Hmm? Oh. Slugs. For the penny slots. . . . A hobby, just. Keeps the dull out of me. I give them to the little ones when I go to town," he said matter-of-factly.

I nodded. The old man was charmingly daft, but too much alone, I sensed.

Leaning across the table, the sailor patted my arm. "Now, don't you move. I'll be right back."

Rummaging about in the lone cupboard, which seemed to define the kitchen area, the old salt returned with an unlabelled blue bottle and two glasses, and smiled.

"Care for a nip then?" he asked with relish. "Do you some good; warm you up just fine, take the shivers right out of you . . ."

Not bothering to await my reply, he topped the

glasses with the thick brown liquid from the bottle. "Want some bitters with that?" he queried. "No? Well, cheers then, lad!" He swallowed the drink half away in one quaff.

"To you, sir," I toasted gravely, taking a tentative sip.

It was very strong and foreign but I savored the peppery aftertaste. I had never tasted anything like it before.

"Parch," I asked, "what do you call these spirits?"

He looked at me as if not understanding my question. "Nip," he finally answered, as if explaining to a simpleton. "Just nip." He took another sip, as did I. And another, and again. With his occasional grunts and groans, his humming, he comforted me, as would a purring cat.

Setting down his cup, he retrieved one of the slugs and set to work again. "It's all I have now—my hobbies. Now, when I was a boy, there was no time for hobbies. . . . Didn't even know what one was till they dry-docked me. Turns out hobbies are what you used to do to get paid for, but now you do them for free, heh. So, when I retired, I moved back, built me a ferry, and there you go. They told me I could live here if I kept an eye to what goes on up yonder"—he gestured toward the cemetery. "*They* don't give me no trouble. Not a one's tried to get out yet."

He wistfully regaled me with tales of his long years at sea in the merchant marine, traveling the world, working his way up the ranks to finally command his own vessel. Whiling away the wet hours in this fashion, the mariner drained his memory, and I helped drain his bottle.

Captain Parch had returned three years ago, and much had changed in the fifty-five years of his absence. He lit his pipe; I enjoyed the pungent smell as he ruminated.

"No sir, isn't the same at all . . . but then, neither am I! When I was young, there was no talk of leaving home, of traveling the world. I just up and did it on my own. Being an orphan, it was good riddance and good luck! But nowadays, it's all the young people talk about—moving out, making a life somewhere else. Anywhere else. It's a crying shame, I tell you. Things have gone wrong for this town, ignoring all what made it great, those little things that add up to something greater. But, you know, it happens everywhere else, too, so maybe it's just an idea in the air, round the world, hey? A bad idea. . . When we lose track of the little things, the big ones follow. I've seen it; it comes with withering speed."

Parch sat back, savoring his jeremiad. The rain had stopped and the afternoon sun soon beamed through the smudged windows of the tiny cabin. The "plink" of the overflowing pot became less and less frequent.

Relaxed and content, I had nothing to add to whatever to Parch was rambling about, simply listening to his drone and nodding in agreement from time to time. Nimbly jumping from one topic to another, he was obviously enjoying himself. But it was now time to take my leave. I stretched and stood, extending my hand again.

The retired sailor took it with some regret. "Ah, sir, it was my pleasure, for certain," he said, leading me to the door. My jacket was unwearable, still soaked and clumped with clods of graphite; I folded it over my arm.

Woozy from the liquor and stiff from sitting, we stepped unsteadily into the fresh cool air. The sun seemed intensely bright and my eyes teared up. I looked to the ground, trying to focus in such brilliance. It dawned on me that the storm had temporarily rinsed away the omnipresent filter of airborne graphite. Thankfully, it would soon return to its usual state. I could smell the ozone from the lightning strikes; it was stimulating.

Rounding the corner of the cabin, a strange sight presented itself: an ancient man, propped upright by a middle-aged woman, was weakly digging in the graveyard.

"Take a good look at that sad sight," directed Parch. "It's the passing of an era."

"How do you mean?" I asked.

"He's the shovel maker for the town, that digger there. Once he plants himself, that's it. There's no one around to take his place. Like I was telling you."

I looked to Parch for an explanation, and with a sad sigh he supplied it.

"It's an old custom here," he said quietly. "Goes way back, but I guess it started to die when I was out to sea. And a shame it is, too. When I was little, it was still the tradition that every newborn was presented with a shovel. Even orphans. A handy tool, to be sure. I still got mine, somewhere . . . but I never knew who gave it to me. Anyway, as I say, a useful tool used for all the usual things by folks. But when their lives were played out, and they knew it, they used it one last time, to dig their own graves. 'Making the bed,' they call it. Guess I'll be making my own before too long, hey?"

I was curious about this peculiar custom. On the hill was a man who should have been in bed dying with dignity; instead, he was here, digging his grave with the last of his earthly energies.

Parch continued: "What with so-called progressive health care and all, folks just get too settled to bother with the tradition. . . . They're too damn old and too damn feeble to handle the task! Oy! And then the kids, they move out looking for better and all. They could care less, anyways. And it's cheaper—and tidier—to be cremated. And the Council—they make it hard on the custom too, pushing metal coffins and such, 'balming and vaults, wanting to be modern like other towns so they can charge the taxes . . ." He turned irate. "The only good thing about those men is they rarely get anything done! Ever. I tell you, sir, you just can't die and fill a hole anymore! You got to be tanned and canned and have permission slips!" He sighed. "Ah, it's a mighty shame."

Perhaps it was the peculiar state of my mind, in combination with the nip; perhaps Parch's rant about progress triggered my thought. As I looked from the shovel maker at his last grim task, and then to the water running downhill to the clay pits, the answer to the puzzle I came here to find revealed itself. I was stunned by the underlying simplicity of the problem. My epiphany was complete.

I realized in my flash of insight that what the factory guide had said was correct: The quality of graphite mined here was the same as ever. But it was the constitution of the clay used in the cores that had changed. It lacked one vital element—the human element.

The old, simple burial customs allowed for the total reabsorption of the body back into nature. The course of water seeking its own level carried the necessary human elements downhill to augment the clay beds, resulting in a unique union: the ideal clay binder for making perfect pencil inserts.

The dwindling population and vanity preservation of the deceased eventually prompted a critical imbalance in the mix. Over the years, the human particles were not sufficiently replaced and these missing ingredients in the clay led to brittleness in the pencil cores. The fragile fusion of unique materials was being undermined by "progress."

In my room I pondered my revelation well into the night, eventually falling into a fitful slumber of disturbing dreams, of which I could recall few details upon waking after noon. The low gray sky portended more wet weather, mirroring my heavy mood. Listless, I decided to visit Parch to say good-bye and set out with umbrella in hand. Paying a call at the apothecary to replace the bottle of nip the two of us had drained the previous day, I proceeded to the lake. The path down to the basin proved slippery and treacherous, slowing my descent as I tested the footing. The light was starting to fade when I finally made secure ground, and I hurried along to the captain's home. While passing the quaint lakeside cottage, I froze in place. The sudden bellow of a large animal in pain broke the silence, and I trembled as I watched the wounded beast crash through the overgrown shrubbery, heading my way. My fear was replaced by anger and disgust when the rampaging bulk blundered into the open, revealing itself to be a corpulent drunkard. Staggering about, he held up his pants with one hand while clasping his jug in the other. The fool wheeled to the front of the cottage. Plopping on the steps with a grunt, he hoisted the jug and took a pull, refilling his recently emptied bladder. I spat in repulsion and anger. Heading for the lights of Parch's hovel, I wondered how such a gross lummox could attain such mass.

I related the disturbing incident to Captain Parch, who shook his head knowingly as he poured out two drams of nip.

"Aye," he muttered. "Too damn many of that type pass this way of late. . . . Some crazier'n loons." Parch produced a blackjack from a back pocket, offering it silently, but I waved it away.

He poured another round and we clinked cups. "One for the road, then, eh? Then off you go, while there's still some light," Parch insisted. "No tellin' what might come out when it's dark, heh?"

I nodded in agreement and drained the cup with one swallow. Saluting the old sea dog with a smile of thanks, I left without another word.

The light was dimming as I hurried down the paved path to the beach. I marched briskly toward the ridge, hoping to make its summit before nightfall. From there, the lights of the town would be my guide. I warily closed on the cottage, scanning the property for movement, listening for a grunt or belch. With my attention thus occupied, I abruptly sprawled head first into the soggy graphite beach, tripped by an unseen obstacle. Jumping up in a panic, I spun around to determine my situation, but I was alone. Breathing deep to slow my pounding heart, I inched toward the source of my fall. I received another start. The obese reason of my intense, if errant, wariness stretched before me in the shallows like a beached whale. I circled the hulk, apprising his condition.

After a moment's reflection, I decided I must have him. Kneeling next to the giant, I clamped my right hand tightly over his mouth, and with my left pinched his nostrils tightly together. When he began struggling to free himself, I increased my pressure and his fight soon stilled, a final shiver playing through the huge body. Nonetheless, I kept my hands firmly in place for several more minutes. Trembling from the effort, I tested his neck for a pulse; it was still. I rose and brushed the clumps of damp graphite from my pants and proceeded quickly to the town in a euphoric state. I breathlessly reported my shocking find on the beach to the town constabulary before returning to the lodge, ordering up a flask of brandy and a bath.

I have never felt so alive and essential as at that moment. In the reconstruction of the clay beds, the bulky body would serve as a cornerstone. I was certain that in death the nameless man would contribute vastly more to history than he ever dreamed of in life—if he dreamed at all. In fact, the passing of the nameless and gluttonous sot inspired me to instigate the project I privately refer to, with intentional irony, as the Last Resort.

Business has been a bit slow here at the Graphite Sanitarium, but it is building. Of the twelve beds currently available, two are occupied by men of ripe age, related but from different branches of an affluent family. One being senile, the other demented, the pair were sequestered here by the family to effectively prevent their meddling in the complicated family intrigues to plunder their personal assets. A middle-aged woman with a dire affliction of the nerves is my third guest. I have a very strong suspicion that the poor creature's end is very near at hand, as her increasingly frequent bouts of unnerving and ear-piercing shrieks in the middle of the night certainly indicate. She was attracted here by the apparent but theoretical restorative qualities to be found the water of Graphite Lake, the positive possibilities of which are considered at length in my circular and advertisements. My first guest was a local charity case I took in, and died two days later. She was interred in one of the plots closest to the lake, as will be all my clients who pass away. That is part of my service package.

After purchasing the lakeside cottage for my enterprise, I commenced its renovation and expansion. My next acquisition—for a nominal fee, paid to the Graphite Community Trust—was the exclusive use, for the duration of the existence of the Sanitarium, of nearly two acres of the least-favored burial sites in the cemetery, being those that slope to the lake. To my thinking, it is prime property, had for the price of its upkeep.

Every afternoon, at 4:35 on the dot, rain or shine, my good friend Parch drops by for a nip or two and a chat. Feisty as ever, the old mariner has plenty of bones to pick to keep him going for quite some time.

I will spend my remaining days in this charming town. Here in Graphite, the true purpose of my life was revealed, and only here can I fulfill my mission. And when the time is near, I will take my place on the hill to make my last bed. In time my parts will mingle with those of generations before me, and I will be reborn as a small but essential element of the finest pencils in the world, recording some of the most profound words ever written, and defining some of the most sublime images ever imagined by man.

Brighter

Damn these filthy pest-birds! Such a nuisance, a twittering plague! Their numbers increase every season—and their stays seems longer and longer. Years past, they would be far south by now, scouring the landscape clean. Like locusts, they are . . . except they eat locusts as well—their only worthwhile trait. They cling to what little purchase they can find on my cocoon, my wrappings, making what time I have left of my mortal life an absolute hell, chirping and squawking and pecking away at my flesh with their sharp blood-sucking beaks. Shoo! Shoo, you dirty things! Oh, damn this outrage! I haven't even the energy to scare them off. Not even the noxious fumes from my cocoon seem to bother them, though the stench makes me ill. My eyes have not stopped watering since I was bound, and now these vile birds peck the frozen tears and the tallow congealed on my face. I think the blighted little bastards are actually *attracted* by the volatile fumes. No doubt, they are a part of my apotheosis to godhood, perhaps a favorable sign, as those candidates who preceded me did not have to suffer this particular humiliation. . . . Hah!

Some raiment for my ascension to the throne—a crown of raucous and ratty little pest-birds, my royal mantle fashioned from the sluice of their foul droppings! I daresay not a single one of my clients would recognize me. Me, the nattiest dresser of all art dealers, the dandy without peer! Once I had dealt with DeFleur, at any rate, he did not wear his clothes well, with that broken body of his. Yes, I am the greatest art dealer, and I await the ultimate test to be the most brilliant artist of my time—perhaps of all time! I left nothing to chance for this trial. I made certain that I would shine the brightest—by paying a quick, quiet, and costly visit to Granatois, the bodybinder for the Proof, in the few hours allotted me before turning myself in for purification. If only these evil birds could be bribed so easily! Behind my back it has been whispered that I am a parasite in the trade; if that is so, then I now serve as the parasitic host to these disgusting feathered monsters. Oh well, I hope they keep to their current perch when I am set alight!........................
....
....

DeFleur demanded perfection from all but himself. But am I not the very epitome of that quality? He surely did recognize and laud excellence, but that lofty ideal was a distant second to his lust for lucre. His quest for perfection was applied primarily to his employees, and few could tolerate the blatant hypocrisy. Ha! Despite DeFleur's discerning eye and scholarship, and his instincts and deep commitment to aesthetic philosophies that have guided the history of art, he utterly overlooked my potential! Little bent man! After a cursory glance at my paintings, he shrugged dismissively and mentioned he had an open position at the moment, caring for his inventory. It would be of value, he suggested, for a young painter to learn the business side of art. Ha! The fool! If he could only see me now!

But at the time I had no choice in the matter, really. My meager resources were exhausted soon after being booted from the studio of that cretin Falibone—of all people!—telling *me:* "Janos Gambon, you are good for nothing but painting signs!" and demanding I leave his service at once. I cannot think of a better example of the blind teaching the sighted to see. And yet the atelier system and its ethos of standardization thrives. The fool blamed *me* for failing to live *down* to his expectations!

DeFleur taught me more in our first meeting than Falibone had in three years, simply by telling me, with a twist of irony, "Young man, just remember this: Never sell your honor twice!" Haha . . . DeFleur should have taken his own advice. Or kept his counsel to himself, as things ultimately played out. And as for *his* opinion of my paintings, I took it too much to heart, for, as I later learned, his crooked body and ruined leg resulted from a beating he received for cheating a young and reckless painter whom DeFleur was promoting. I suspect the brutal thrashing he received led to his dealing only in vintage works by long-dead artists. The trade was certainly more lucrative—and dead artists have little fight. The decrepit clientele who collected such art retaliated only with writs and lawsuits. DeFleur, of course, retained the best legal heroes in the field, his soldiers who, at his direction, would draw out the suits as long as possible, seemingly forever. He considered such disputes a

war of attrition. The few cases that were found against DeFleur, as much as they grieved him, were infinitely preferable to a painful and deforming fight. I am absolutely certain DeFleur deserved every blow delivered him by the angry young painter, and probably more.....
....
....
....
....
....
....
....
....

On rare occasions, DeFleur would ask how my painting was progressing, motivated by the sheer boredom of a dead Saturday afternoon, or a sudden inspiration of politeness, or, most likely, making certain I was not making strides that would free me from his thrall. But I always found these moments gratifying, considering them as acknowledgments, of a sort.

All those years drudging in DeFleur's painting storage, caring for the artworks, assisting in showings, taking the blame for errors of my underlings as the business expanded, silently suffering his demeaning comments in the presence of royalty and the wealthy for my inability to be in two places at once. . . I could waste the few hours left to me listing the indignities I endured in the service of the old cheat. And yet I stayed, the compensation sufficient to survive on a fairly comfortable level, though the schedule left me but one day a week to recuperate and, if sufficiently motivated, to work on my paintings, of which I had completed a small but personally satisfying group. DeFleur, on dull summer Saturdays, would sometimes engage me in conversations to relieve his ennui, and seemed to appreciate some of the insights I expressed about gallery works that intrigued me. I was quietly pleased to subsequently hear some of my points used by the old dog in his efforts to sell said works. He seemed to develop over time a grudging respect for my opinions, though he took much greater delight in proving me wrong or simply dismissing my comments as idiotic blather. During slow periods, if I was current with my work, he never badgered my whiling away dead work hours in the gallery library—one of the most compendious in private hands—from which I borrowed ideas for my personal work. In this way, and over time, we came to an uneasy and grudging regard for each other, though I despised his callous abuse until realizing that he considered everyone an inferior and thus discovered his fatal flaw, the chink in his armor...

....
....
....
....
....
....
....
....
....
....
....
....
....
....
....
....
....

Oh, such a horror, the great strife. It began with that unsavory blind sculptor and his flinty personality that sparked the conflagration that followed. Yes, Maruna Godulfus—thoroughly unpleasant in every respect, uncouth and arrogant, and yet he possessed a very real power over women. An incredible artist, undoubtedly, whose work will be remembered and revered for generations to come. His portrait busts are flawless works in marble and bronze—every imperfection exactingly in place, every wrinkle and charm, no matter how trivial, was rendered accurately for posterity. But his unusual working process finally did him in. Being sightless, he would run his hands over the surface of the sitter that was to be sculpted, for days on end, until the image was recorded in what he referred to as his tactile memory. Once satisfied that he had absorbed sufficient information, he would then set to work, either in clay, from which a mold would be pulled for an eventual bronze casting, or by chiseling the sculpture from a block of marble. His hands would constantly "read" the work surface in a search for flaws, that is, information not recorded in his tactile memory, and in need of refinement, correction, or deletion.

Godulfus was of small stature and of bulky build, and was very strong. Despite his ugly temper and lack of hygiene, and due to the intimacy of his process and his reputation for exacting reproduction, he was sought by many of the celebrated beauties of the day, so that their vanity would be recorded faithfully for history, and their comeliness immortalized by his talent and skill. Inevitably, in the process of tactilely memorizing his subjects, many of them fell in love with his sensitive touch, which was said to be indescribable, a hallowed subject to be exclusively discussed among the company of the sculptor's sitters. No surprise that his sittings with ripe fair ladies took much longer than those of his male subjects! He brazenly took advantage of these situations, and made many enemies from the cuckolded husbands and betrayed lovers. The uncomfortably sensual nude portrait bust that resulted from the sittings of Thodorea, wife of the prominent painter and Formalist leader, Pokolo Plomatea—and the sculptor's obscene boasting of her seduction—proved to be his undoing and served as the flashpoint of the bloody conflict between the Formalist and the Romantic artists. That is a fact. Fat artists, under the sudden financial strain of the disastrous fall of the economy, promoted their typical pointless philosophical sniping into a full-scale war, and the blatant ravishing of Madame Plomatea by Godulfus, while a personal insult to her stern husband, became a critical issue of dispute between the groups. But my! She *is* such a lovely one! I can hardly blame Godulfus—I would have paid plenty to fill his shoes then!

I'm certain that Pokolo was wounded when Thodorea chose Godulfus over a Formalist sculptor for the bust. But the blind sculptor risked much more than he meant to wager with his loud and indiscreet bragging of the affair while on a long drunk. The sculptor's lewd recounts of the affair rubbed Pokolo's nose in his wife's infidelity and such baiting demanded a response. Nor did it help that Pokolo's wayward wife twittered to her inner circle about the ecstasy provided by Godulfus. These words, too, spread quickly, and the scandal became the *only* talk of the town, the particulars growing more grotesque with every retelling. Pokolo's hand was forced. Godulfus, the querulous gadabout with a harsh word for all who crossed his path, went suddenly absent, to the relief of many, though some surmised that he had come to his senses once sober, taking a holiday to let hot tempers cool. Only the naïve put any stock in that suggestion. The mystery of the sculptor's disappearance was solved several days later when the night watch discovered a naked decapitated body in the town square at dawn. Identification was verified when the head of Godulfus was found neatly sewn into his rectum.

Due to the clever stitch-work on the sculptor's posterior, it wasn't long before the local sleuths cast an eye of suspicion on the tailors' guild. What the guilds' motives would be, I haven't the faintest idea—except that the victim was a fashion abomination. Grilledge, in the course of fitting me for a striking new suit of cobalt blue velvet, told me of the visit paid him that very morning by two of the bumbling town constables. He declared he was absolutely *shocked* they were able to track him down. I had such a laugh, haha, his shop being but three doors down from their headquarters.

Retaliation by the Romantic artists was the inevitable. Due to the harsh economic climate, the artists had few opportunities to exhibit and sell, and too much time to brood and drink and bravely boast of honor. Hard times and extreme actions bring out the worst in artists. Violence breeds more violence, with its mindless hatred spreading like fire through a library. That Godulfus—he was something else altogether. . . . But his . . . work . . . it is . . . truly . . . genius..................................
....
....
....
....
....
....

O-oo-oo-oo! The cold! Unbearable! Not only is this a trial of fire, but of ice as well. Where are those damned pest-birds now? I *need* their relentless worrying, to relieve the itch in my cheek. Ahh! It's driving me utterly mad! Eh? Hello! What is that? Is someone coming my way? Over there, a boy! He's heading for town, to begin his apprenticeship, hopefully *not* under the faulty ministrations of that master-bastard Falibone. Yoo-hoo, boy!

Young man! Over here . . . look up . . . higher, lad! Do not fear, I am the greatest of artists. . . . Wait! Stop! Do you hear? There is no need to run away. But can he even hear me? What do I sound like, so weak and limp? Am I just muttering strange noises? My tongue is so dry. . . . Don't go, I just need a favor of you, please? I would be ever so grateful. Please, if you can just fetch a branch, a long one, to scratch my cheek with, one that will reach, if you will? Wait! Stop! Damn. I scared him off. He refused to look my way, just covered his eyes with one hand and with the other warded me off with the sign of the evil eye. . . . I must be quite a sight to the uninitiated, though: a face poking out of a monstrous black and stinking cocoon bound to a six-meter stake. Oh, how long must I wait for my passage to eternal eminence? It is so damned cold. But maybe it will freeze this damned itch...
....
....
....
....
....
....

I feel so weak—I might not even survive the few hours till my Proof! And with this bitter cold, my frozen face may very well freeze and break, falling away in pieces.

Brighter

So tired. . . . Ah, those mortifying cleansing rituals in preparation for the contests. After ten days of fasting with only an occasional cup of water, I would have gratefully wolfed down a bucket of dirt. Posthumo's tepid cup of worm gruel was a feast. At that point in my preparation, after ten days, there is nothing—*nothing!*—I would reject as sustenance..................................
....
....
....
....
....
....
....
....
....
....
....
....
....
....
....
....
....
....
....
....
....
....
....
....
....
....
....
....
....
....
....
....

....
....
....
....
....
....
....
....
....
....
....
....

What am I doing here? Why in hell did I *agree* to such a barbaric practice? Am I *insane*? Letting my vanity carry me into this ridiculous, this *barbaric* suicide! Somebody, anybody—please take me down. This is a mistake—a case of mistaken identity! This is a case of vanity . . . nothing more. This action is a proof only of my pride! . . . Someone, please . . . I am not worthy..
....
....
....
....
....
....
....
....
....
....
....
....
....

Oh, such a beautiful thing! So awe-inspiring, *just* like when it happened. The faint silvery tinkling of the bells, the way they gently nudged me from my dream, now just as then, so wonderful, and being irresistibly drawn up and out to the source, vaguely aware of all the others doing the same, joining as one . . . such a warm sense of vital communion. Heeding the call, we assumed our place among every man, woman, and child of Rawwoody to complete a perfect circle that touched the five points of the paved pentagon of the town plaza, to behold the strange originator who beckoned: an ancient naked man whose hoary hair reached his knees, performing elaborate and repetitive gestures with his emaciated limbs and expressive hands, each long thin finger tipped with a tiny silver bell. Muttering exhortations to the heavens in a guttural unknown language, spinning and dipping with mesmerizing grace. He suddenly stopped, frozen in place for an eternity; then with a spiraling move, he gracefully collapsed into a pile in the center of the commons. The vacuum of silence slowly flooded with wavering golden light as the rising sun topped the tree line—it seemed nearly liquid, a slow, glowing syrup that spread everywhere at once, as if it was the actual *illumination* we were seeing, not that which is *illuminated*. And it was so—*beautiful*. Alive and pulsing, somehow *palpable*, and every witness at that moment was in utter awe and in complete empathy. The hairy man slowly rose and tottered unsteadily in a small circle, trying to regain his balance, slowing to a halt. Throwing his thin arms skyward, he spoke in a ringing voice, and I remember the words exactly:

"I am called Posthumo, and bring to you the will of the uncounted suns that keep the horror of the void at bay. For five years, I have traveled to deliver these words, to which you must not only listen but also hear. You have perverted your gifts of enlightenment, using your talents for murder and conflict, spilling blood and creating fear to acquire trivial power. Those who do not tolerate difference are condemned to indifference. Indifference is the essence of the void.

"I have been sent to illuminate the darkness that has infested and corrupted your destinies and lives, your histories. You must obey the celestial demands that I speak—*me*, a mere puppet made of filth—to generate the singular light you were born to create. It is written, and so it must be, that the greatest and the mightiest burn the brightest, and shall take their rightful place among the many suns that shine aloft in the night. The light is the Truth and fire is the Proof. Thus, the trials of fire and light must begin, and I will guide you along the only path of your salvation."

The purpose of his presence delivered, the mystic sank slowly into a cross-legged sit, hands folded into the basket of his naked lap. Once free of Posthumo's thrall, the crowd was disoriented and puzzled. I was confused, the crowd around me buzzed with quiet but anxious whispers, and there in the middle of the town pentagon sat the evidence of the experience.

Rattled by the uninvited tourist, the magistrates shrugged and nodded furiously in a huddle of threatened self-importance, haha. Emphatic gestures punctuated their cross-conversations, one member or another periodically raising his head to make certain Posthumo did not attempt to slip away after his unauthorized and unsettling announcement. The town constabulary surrounded the ascetic, throwing a sere cloak over his naked shoulders before gently leading him away without a hint of resistance. By noon that day, a rumor spread throughout the town. After hours of intense and repetitive interrogation meant to trip up the old man, Posthumo patiently answered that he was sent by the stars to oversee a terrible contest between the two factions of artists as the only resolution to the rift. The magistrates were seriously considering the legality of the proposal and, via messenger, had sent it on to the provincial authorities for their legal opinion. It was quietly inferred that the hermit exercised a persuasive influence over those in his immediate vicinity, his arguments and demands deemed credible by all in his presence. If DeFleur owned such powers, he would own every penny in the world, and the loudest mouth to let all know it!

But DeFleur had his particular powers. Ah, what an eye, and true scholarship and insight, not only into the souls of the deceased artists, but also into the hearts and wallets of the late artists' alive and well-heeled patrons. He had genius and an unerring sense of custodianship, making certain his prime treasures went to the best collections, the owners of which had enough passion or conceit, and, of most import, had qualifying bankers of repute. The other paintings were sold first come, first served—along with the same requisite resources. Haha, all patrons were treated as equals, though the famously wealthy always came first! And the stupid rich—they were a dealer's dream come true, paying the ridiculous

asking prices without a haggle, so anxious were they for the social cache such goods bestow. But DeFleur, the old goat, saved many a masterpiece by his careful placement, craftily using rare works as leverage to gain direct access to the private and discreet wealthy. Those were the lessons I learned in my first week as stock boy at DeFleur's shop. They opened my eyes and put me to sleep at the . . . same . . . time................................
....
....
....
....
....
....
....
....
....
....
....
....
....
....

Ah no! No! What ugliness! So . . . *uncouth*! Terrible acts were committed against the Formalist camp by Romantic fanatics, in retaliation for the murder of Godulfus. In the name of *Godulfus*! Who would have thought his murder would engender such acts? Godulfus was universally despised by one and all. Anyone who knew him, even casually, had wished him dead at one time or another—with the exception of his corps of lovers. Either camp would have been proud to claim his work, if not necessarily the maker, and could convincingly argue the sculptor's legacy belonged with them. The idiosyncratic sculptor was a true individualist, incorporating facets of each philosophy. Godulfus died for publicly gloating about pinning the wife of the Formalist leader, and the action against him contained a tiny seed of justification, but it also served as the perfect excuse the Romantics needed to prove that they, too, were entitled to exact justice and, in the process, make their own metaphorical statements. Their choice of victims, however, was an incredible mistake.

The Formalists Lorga Botch and Maren Darlu—two of the most influential, and venerable, of the Formalist painters, were murdered at some point following the inaugural evening and festivities of their dual retrospective at the Rotunda, Rawwoody's stately museum and exhibition hall. The exhibition was wonderful, of highest quality, and included works from every period, highlighting the influence each had on the other as they pursued shared ideals. To the untrained eye, their works appear to be identical, but a closer inspection reveals the particular quirks that have always defined their difference. That the entire town was looking forward with joy to this major exhibition honoring two of the most loved and highly esteemed painters of their generation barely states the case; these two artists, lovers since before anyone could remember, were the grandfathers of all disciplines and philosophies and indeed, every artist in town—they were sympathetic and supportive to all, fostering even the like of Godulfus. They gave of themselves freely, without any thought of reward in return. The insult they ultimately received froze the blood of most in the town. Outrage and demands for justice and retribution emerged once the numbing shock of their murders dissipated—quite the opposite from the sense of deliverance that the murder of Godulfus seemed to inspire.

The exhibition was a low-key affair, at Maren and Lorga's request, for they were sensitive to the growing friction between the two camps—several beatings had been reported, none too dire, but untended sparks can lead to conflagrations. Though the featured artists counted many close friends among the Romantics, the tension between the groups was such that it was wiser, and safer, for some of their friends to stay home altogether. The more aggressive wing of the Romantics, however, organized a noisy and obnoxious demonstration in an attempt to ensure that anyone crossing the line to visit the enemy did not have an enjoyable evening but, rather, one fraught with threats. Most of the casual public wisely refrained from attending. The Formalists appeared en masse, however, in a strong showing of support for their heroes, and much spitting and skirmishes and similar acts of rudeness ensued as the Romantics sought to disrupt the proceedings. As chance would have it, my arrival coincided with that of the Formalists. It proved to be an unfortunate occasion to introduce my cobalt blue velvet suit in public, as Grephe Loke, a Romantic sculptor, fouled the shoulder of my long jacket with an errant gob of his phlegm. With disgust, I dabbed away the sputum with my kerchief and took two strides to where he stood. He stammered his apologies, for he was under consideration for the gallery I was planning. But, waving a hand for his silence, I pressed the kerchief to his stained jerkin, where it stayed, fixed in place by the glue of his own manufacture. "Keep this as a reminder, as it is all you will ever get from me," I said flatly before resuming my entrance.

The constabulary, not of sufficient number, was barely able to keep the partisans from the throats of their rivals; upon the arrival of the last of the invited stragglers, the museum's doors were closed. As the town watch remained, the Romantic troublemakers soon drifted away. A sedate dinner for the honored artists, attended by their closest friends and collectors, followed the ceremonies at the Rotunda. Little energy suffused the table and the honored pair seemed preoccupied. The crude protests had cast a pall over the whole affair and all were relieved when the evening ended soon after the dinner.

The next morning, the night watch discovered the lifeless, nude, and defiled corpses of Maren and Lorga, their limbs and backbones so battered and broken that the crushed bodies sagged into the rhythm of the grand stairs leading up to the plaza of the Rotunda. Twisted versions of formalist platitudes had been carved into their torsos. *Nature is the tonic of logic*—I remember that one. Their masterful paintings, icons of order and reason, now reduced to ragged and ripped linen, splintered wood and broken frames, littered the plaza as if spewed from the great doors of the museum, which gaped dark and wide. The Romantics had claimed the glove thrown by the Formalists, and with it slapped their arrogant rivals.

The community was shocked by the brutality of the crime, and the magistrates called in all art dealers that had so far survived the economic collapse that had decimated the art world—perhaps one-third the number as six months previous. Emerging from my self-imposed retirement following DeFleur's death, I attended as an unaffiliated dealer. The dealers were no help, nearly broke and most hanging by a thread. Penniless and with few prospects of success on any level, the artists sought security in the company of allies, their collective frustration ripe for eruption..................................
....
....
....
....
....
....

Damn Posthumo, with his fasts, his glisters, and his purgatives! He certainly left me a clean and empty vessel for infusion of the Almighty. Ha. The distant roll of thunder heard in Rawwoody is merely the desperate growl of demand vented by my starved stomach. . . . If fortunate enough to be offered one, I swear I would eat

a porcupine. Alive. . . . Light? . . . Am I on fire? . . . The moon! The moon on the rise! My time will be soon. I can see so far, all the way across the valley. . . . Ugh—do *not* look down! You are *securely* bound to this stake. . . . Eyes forward, Gambon, straight ahead, man! Close your eyes and . . . keep them shut. Block out the light . . . dark . . . peaceful...
....
....
....
....
....
....
....
....
....
....
....
....
....

Following the murders of Maren and Lorga, the carnage between the artists increased dramatically. No soothsayer was needed to predict the violence that would ruin what was left of the art market, or that troubling and hard times lay ahead for the painters and sculptors. The future bleak and threatening, they took their frustrations out on each other, rival dogs of the same pack...........
....
....
....
....
....

What weighty event most influenced the scales of my life? Without doubt, it was the opening reception of the exhibition of Ardent Loflow, *The Northern Pasbabaratta*, that ridiculously massive and unconvincing overview launched by DeFleur at the gallery. Loflow was no Pasbabaratta, by any stretch, but DeFleur had collected his work avidly over the years, especially after the artist's death, when it was plentiful and cheap. He purchased mostly from auctions, and then from the family directly once he tracked them down, thus evading the auction's commission for the sale. He *so* resented paying that. . . . DeFleur eventually accumulated some 400 paintings, and twice that number of works on paper. Once ready, he launched the first retrospective of the artist's work, touting the exhibition with a flattering and pompous broadside commissioned from an art scholar, at one time of some reputation but who now wrote what he was hired to write. Such a farcical and fraudulent enterprise!

The combined framing and restoration expense was twice the purchase price of the paintings and DeFleur's asking price twenty times the cumulative costs of each work. Everyone who was anyone showed up, the opening being wisely scheduled on a slow social weekend. DeFleur kept the wine servers circling to refill even half-empty glasses, creating quite the gala occasion for such a menial artist. I was quite heady myself when I heard angry voices rising above the merry din, and the guests quickly quieted to listen and lean into the center of the row. Curson, the buying agent of the gallery, and DeFleur were engaged in a loud and bitter bicker. Curson was ranting about DeFleur cheating him out of commissions, while DeFleur screamed his innocence and threatened Curson with legal action for public defamation. DeFleur was certainly not above clipping his own employees if given the opportunity, as I had witnessed on several occasions over the years.

Plied with drink, I acted, quick and sure, informing the hired door attendants that Curson was not to be readmitted once he departed, under any condition. I hurried to the center of the argument, pulling Curson away to whisper in his ear that a messenger sent by his wife said that his daughter had taken a turn for the worse and was very ill. I knew from eavesdropping that his daughter Loraline was sickly. Curson's face went white at the news. Contemptuously pushing a vulgar hand gesture in DeFleur's face, he left for home and his little Loraline. DeFleur called for wine! Music! The magic words bellowed, the party was on once again. DeFleur clapped me on the back. "That was brilliant!" he crowed, laughing with relief. "On Monday, Jano, I want to speak with you about a position that has opened up." We clinked glasses. *That* was the tipping point of my life.

Yes, that was *the* significant moment in my personal situation, but it fortuitously coincided with the emergence of an unforeseen—I might even say *unseen*—clientele: the ambitious and educated progeny of prosperous merchants. I first noticed their presence at the auctions, dreary affairs usually attended by penny-pinching dealers and the hopeful but strapped consignors. The newcomers immediately caught my attention: well dressed and raucous, bidding aggressively on favored lots, they had a merry time, win or lose. I made a point of trumping their bids—not only to gauge how high they were willing to go, but also to gain their attention by winning

every lot of contention. After driving up the price on a fine Gobetta, I dropped out and let my young rival take it. He absolutely beamed with satisfaction when the gavel fell. Introducing myself to the lively crew at the conclusion of the sale, I congratulated my bidding rival on his wise purchase. Taking the lot to Café Woy-Ardor for a drop or two, I invited them to a private viewing at the gallery that weekend. DeFleur was not pleased to hear this but my smart little group proved the life of the party. DeFleur spent most of the evening surrounded by bright young ladies, entertaining them with his salty war stories. I took on the cadre as my project, tutoring them, refining their taste, and becoming the guiding light of this new social set. My disciples provided me entrée to the newly wealthy, who craved the social status of the old guard. Ha. Yes! I was a necessary fixture in this hedonistic social scene. . . . Oh, those were some of the best years of my life! I think. . . . If I could only remember more of those years................................
....
....
....
....
....
....
....
....

....
....
....
....
....
....
....
....
....
....
....
....
....
....
....
....
....

The Rawwoody officials consulted the Provincial High Court for legal clarification and guidance regarding Posthumo's sinister demand for Proof by trials of fire, but the matter was quickly thrown back into laps of the local authorities. No legal precedent existed on which to rule out such a harsh resolution, nor was there one to allow it. Since the conflict was peculiar to the town and its inhabitants, the court granted it permission to act as the local judiciary thought best. The province ordered the filing of a detailed report of all events and remedies taken by the town in the remedy of this perplexing matter. Empowered but puzzled, the local government embarked with trepidation on a path leading straight into the flames, ratifying Posthumo's dire solution unanimously and with little discussion. I was asked to serve as head of a panel of art professionals, acting as liaison between the artist factions and the judicial tribunal, which would oversee the actions demanded by Posthumo. I could hardly turn down the appointment, as it offered me an intimate view of the whole bizarre drama as it unfolded. It was also the perfect opportunity to emerge from my self-imposed fallow period following my triumphant intrigue against DeFleur.

Two days later, I was called to a meeting of the art factions' leaders, the Rawwoody court, and Posthumo. The old hermit was most persuasive, I must say, and though uttering few words, he established the essential outline of the trials of the Proof. The meeting lasted till late afternoon and by sundown the agreement was common knowledge throughout town: all parties agree that the dispute between the artists shall be settled by a contest of fire and light between champions from each camp, who will be determined by the drawing of lots. Both contestants are to report to Posthumo after a final hour with their families. Posthumo would oversee the strict regimen, for the period of two weeks, to ready and purify the contestants for their trial. The judgment of

the brightest burned artist would be determined by objective mechanical means, if available, and if not, by Posthumo. The lottery was to take place in two days, at noon. The contest would be held the night of the next full moon—two weeks to the day. I demanded of my gallery artists that they stay clear of any involvement with either group and, though factional sympathies ran deep with them, they offered only token resistance. Quickly reverting to form, they picked only at each other. What I found strangest of all was the deafening silence from the town clergy, so intimidated were they by Posthumo and his deep beliefs and harrowing trials. Cowed like the rest of us, they awaited the result of the upcoming Proof before venturing any opinions or statements about the situation.......................................
....
....
....
....
....
....
....
....

All those late nights at DeFleur's feet—literally sitting at his feet, like a damned dog! So humiliating! Correcting in the harshest terms my attempts to please him, or if not that, at least to not anger him, during my tutelage in his larcenous methods and general chicanery. Then spending extra hours—my hours—listening to his insulting criticism. I nearly went deaf from his harangues! Any small success I stumbled into birthed stern warnings about the dangers of pride. But after a year, I gained DeFleur's confidence, and a measure of respect, and the game of buying and selling paintings became more interesting. The traps set for unwitting clients—complicated and long-term affairs—often resulted in triumph. The art business was a chess game, I finally learned, and subtlety and patience were the cardinal virtues for the cardinal sinners. At receptions all over town, he introduced me to the most influential elements of high society: the wealthy, the royal, and the powerful. After my apprenticeship, DeFleur paid me very well indeed, with commissions and an expense account to boot. In my first year, I accounted for nearly 40 percent of the gallery's sales; in my second year, I pulled more than 60 percent. DeFleur was quite satisfied with me, his invention, and rewarded my efforts on his behalf with the occasional handsome bonus. These were heady times, sparked by the application of new methods of industrial production, which greatly reduced the cost of manpower. The economic index of the province steadily climbed, fueled by the smoky industries of Castaphon and the iron-ore pits of Glambora; no end to the success was in sight. I was the darling of the new rich—a young, suddenly wealthy and flashy set. I was of their ilk and quickly became an essential presence for successful and gaudy revels—decadent affairs that would have been shameful the next morning but for the fact the one scheduled for that evening promised to be even more scandalous. I was the torchbearer for these brilliant barbarians and reveled in all they represented. Especially their money...

....

....

....

....

....

....

....

....

....

....

....

....

....

....

....

....

....

....

....

....

....

....

....

....

What time can it possibly be? When, when will my moment come? The wait is killing me! I may not even last to partake in my glorious death. My face is frozen. . . . Hurry, please! It is too cold . . . and too long a wait......
....
....
....
....
....
....
....
....
....
....
....
....
....
....
....
....
....
....
....
....
....
....
....
....
....
....
....
....
....
....
....
....
....
....
....
....
....
....

....
....
....
....
....
....
....
....
....
....
....
....
....
....
....
....
....
....
....
....
....

I was perplexed at the time that every artist involved in the war volunteered to compete in the Proofings. . . . I thought it demented to be willing to die for art—instead of *living* for it—but now I think I understand..............
....
....
....
....
....
....
....
....

I so loved the idea of being the hero, the center of attention to a group of fawning and well-heeled sycophants. My every whim indulged, my every suggestion generating the fact . . . the perfect clientele for an increasingly imperfect art dealer! Ha! But what was one to do? I was working long, hard hours . . . but little time, if any at all, on my painting, alas, depriving mankind of my divine visions in my quest for increasingly outlandish entertainments. Weekends were lost in waves of pleasure and dissipation and so many days, barely recorded in my memory, were spent pursuing clients and acquiring property, leading to more and more money, but the cost becoming more expensive than profits gained . . . and in pursuit of what, Gambon? Fame? Infamy, perhaps. My reputation soured as my exotic indulgences escalated. It was simply the idiot thrill of gaining more money. Dizzy and deluded, the entire art market thought it would never end. But it did, unexpectedly, and oh, so fast!

The coal miners, ultimately, caused the disaster—though the cartel of coal barons which controlled the Ahol Mines must bear some of the liability, demanding an extra three hours a day more from miners already working twelve-hour shifts to fuel the demands of the metal factories in nearby Castaphon. The owners pushed the miners over the line by refusing to negotiate extra pay for extra hours' work. Outraged by the cartel's arrogance, an extreme faction refused to leave the mine at the end of their shift and barred entry to their replacements. The barons answered the challenge by walling up the shaft entry with rubble, to starve the rebels out, or smother them. The trapped miners, facing certain death in or out, set fire to the shaft and perished as martyrs to their fellows outside. Smart investors began selling off large shares at this point, when the price was still high and before word spread, soon triggering a panic in the market as values tumbled perilously. The honeycomb of shafts made it impossible to quell the relentless flames, which soon reduced the entire site to a smoldering waste. On my visit to Castaphon, I saw the huge murky cloud of doom hanging twenty clicks away, the burn then in its eighteenth month and threatening adjacent mines. The source of energy that fueled the economic boom was evaporating as choking smoke.

The collapse of the industrial index devastated the entire province and beyond. It flattened the luxuries market quickly, with collecting art being a hobby of a privileged few. In Rawwoody, the clap of gallery doors closing was deafening; within three months, the art trade was in shambles. DeFleur, whatever his faults, was an optimistic cheat, and though grievously stricken by the reversal of fortune, he nonetheless forged onward, seeking a new wrinkle to exploit. Ruthlessly trimming the bloated staff hired during the surging market, DeFleur pared it down to a skeleton crew. I was one of the few remaining but essential bones. When the old bilker finally hatched a plan, the burden to execute it fell to me. DeFleur charged me to secure the Gormona collection, a trove of old master paintings of legendary status and long considered untouchable. The few clients not decimated by the economy's precipitous fall—several of whom had actually *benefited* from the disaster—were in a position to drive a hard bargain and exact a degree of revenge for DeFleur's instinctual gouging. DeFleur, of course, sensed this immediately, and factored such necessary false satisfaction into the asking prices.

The paintings were of impeccable provenance, assembled in the previous century by Aramo Gormona, an industrialist from Mute Warren, who made his fortune in the manufacture of metal goods. Most of the paintings originated from royal collections—either lucre for the spendthrift dukes or pieces accepted in partial trade for iron goods, such as cannon, from aggressive despots looking to expand their borders. That was the accepted but never confirmed rumor. The collection of twenty masterworks was legendary, for only a handful of aficionados were granted the privilege to view and study the paintings over the four generations that the Gormona family hoarded them. Aramo soon after moved the family seat to Castaphon to personally oversee his factories. Ugh! Castaphon! Such filth and stink—and the constant ear-bursting noise is unbearable. A disagreeable mix of the exceptionally wealthy and the most desperate poor comprise the population, and the simmering class struggle periodically erupts, resulting in violence and riots.

Gormona's idle offspring lacked their father's vision, ambition, and discipline, and such was the decadent luxury in which they wallowed that not a single heir of any merit was produced. The lot of them was not much good for anything but throwing away the vast fortune, at which they excelled, until the family dwindled to this last effete wastrel, holed up in the estate which housed the collection. The fool had waited too long to sell but nonetheless demanded prices that would have set records at the height of the market. DeFleur was beside himself; I have never seen him in such an agitated state before. His business was failing and he was in debt to a horde of consignors he could not possibly pay off. This was his last desperate chance to salvage his honor and whatever was left of his business . . . and then retire, as he told me frankly. The pressures were wearing on his health and he lacked the energy to continue in a field fraught with so many potential pitfalls. But this was also the biggest and most risky gamble that he had ever chanced and, as all lay in the balance, he found the excitement of the game to be extremely seductive. DeFleur carefully and quietly intimated to the several potential buyers that were approached that he had tied up the collection, and those chosen few discreetly responded positively, inquiring as to when a viewing could be arranged. Though he could not afford any fouled negotiations, DeFleur was resistant to the cash demands of the decadent owner. I insisted that the deal be straight cash for the works, as the heir had demanded. Any argument at this point over the method of payment would jeopardize the entire arrangement and all would be lost. Chagrined though he was, DeFleur finally acquiesced and turned over to me the purchase contracts he had drawn up by his legal representatives, along with a bag of ill-gotten cash from very liquid and unrecorded sales. He handed me the satchel without any demand of my signing a receipt, as he wanted no trail of his chicanery.

To this point in my career, my decline had been gradual but steady; now, standing on the edge of a moral chasm, I did not hesitate to leap and seize my opportunity. I paid a visit to the printer, then stopped by Ho-Lee Sinn's, the *chinee* apothecary. Preparations completed, I climbed up and into a massive sleeper coach I had hired—it just simply would not do to arrive in anything less than an eight-horse carriage, in which my kidneys were luxuriously battered black and royal blue. One would think that at this point in history—the very *height* of civilization—some mechanical genius could produce a smoother method of travel, though I must say that the small but well-appointed privy was a blessing. We made good time, arriving on the outskirts of Castaphon in just over a day's time. Unfortunately, our destination lay beyond the far side of the town, and we were forced to make our slow way through the center. The abominable squalor, block after sooty block, was depressing and endless. The mind-jarring blasts from the furnaces and hammering clangs of huge stamping presses forced me to use my sound blockers. It was odd that major industrial factories dominated the center of Castaphon; in my experience, large factories were located outside the town proper. Then it struck me that the *entire town* was a massive factory. Ramshackle housing erected for the laborers was jammed into whatever space was available between the hulking foundries and mills—reducing tardiness and conserving the energy spent in travel for their jobs. Seeing generation after generation of anonymous working families rarely moving outside the cramped and crowded company-owned slum sent a shiver up my spine. I imagined their empty lives, the infernal, reeking, deafening hours on end, day after day after day, relentlessly, until, finally used up, their children filled the vacancy. Faced with such hopeless prospects, I would throw myself into a cauldron of molten metal on the first day. Castaphon inspires only such thoughts! But with the coal reserves nearly depleted, their current suffering would soon end, to be replaced with starvation and empty prospects. Turning to my plan for relief, I reviewed it

again, making certain it was perfect but for the actual execution. It was *all* I thought about until finally arriving at the Gormona estate. The game was on............
....
....
....
....
....
....
....
....
....
....
....
....
....
....
....
....

When I arrived for the Proof meeting convened before the magistrates, Posthumo and the two representatives of the leadership from each artists' group were already present. I babbled an apology for my tardiness, explaining that an important meeting with my legal representatives regarding my new gallery ran long, haha—but actually I was at the tailor's, being fitted for the scarlet moleskin vest that both Grilledge and I agreed was the perfect complement to my new antelope brown hatched-tweed suit, giving it a dash of pepper. The cost of mole hides—ridiculous! But worth it.

The court had issued an order to submit by signed

lots the members of the respective artists' camps willing to participate in the Proof trial. The leader of each faction would draw the name of the respective champion: first, the cold cuckold Plomatea for the Formalist group, then Lofus Shagafe of the Romantics. Lofus, a dissipated misanthrope, had only recently appeared before the court on charges of rape alleged by an apprentice, but the case was quickly settled out of court. Plomatea chose first. Unfolding the chosen ballot, he stared in silence at what he held, until a court officer pulled the slip away, handing it to the head magistrate, whose eyebrows peaked as he glanced at it. In a sepulchral tone he announced that Pokolo Plomatea would represent the Formalists. The court sternly censured the rival's malicious cackling. Still sniggering, Lofus plunged his hand into the hopper, and drew the ticket of the Romantic's hero. Opening the lot with a sneer quickly stifled, his body visibly trembling, as did his voice upon softly intoning his own name. The court officer pulled the ticket, relaying it to the Judge, who verified to the assembled that Lofus Shagafe was the rival contestant. A queasy thrill coursed through my body and my skin puckered with gooseflesh at the revelation, a reaction I sensed in most of the assembled. I stole a peek at Posthumo but he gazed only at the floor. The two leaders were given one hour with their families and were then to report to the Tribunal for delivery to the mystic. Plomatea morosely followed the court order, but a good six hours passed before the constabulary tracked down Lofus with a pack of dogs that easily followed his pungent scent to a notorious tavern on the edge of town. After a brief scuffle, he was bound and handed over to Posthumo. Both of the chosen were spirited away by the mystic for spiritual counseling, and he supervised the water fast of seven days to purify their bodies, to be followed by a seven-day diet of worms for their sublimation into earth. Posthumo tended as well as he might to their spiritual needs, both contestants being rather worldly.

The artist problem dominated the talk in Rawwoody, and the average citizen had not a clue of the underlying aesthetic rift that separated the groups. Nor would they have *comprehended* the differences if explained to them. The townsfolk were aware the artists were of a different breed, headstrong and eccentric, guided by elusive and esoteric instincts. But their speculations on the cause of the conflict missed the essential point. Their violent

actions of late were based on a need to retaliate, in some way, against the threat of impending poverty and an uncertain future—very common concerns, based on simple survival. Additionally, I believe all artists, regardless of their personal inclination for any school of thought, share a common internal conflict, the friction of which affects their behavior and decisions. Are not all visual artists compelled to see *and* display, to be passive and active simultaneously? Alas, artists are, at once, both voyeurs and exhibitionists. The struggle to keep these contradictory impulses in equitable balance is the root cause of much of their emotional conflicts. Yes. That is *my* theory...
....
....
....
....
....
....
....
....
....
....
....
....
....
....

The sun was setting when the hack rumbled up the circle to the rambling, shabby mansion of the Gormona clan. I climbed out of the coach and stretched. The rough ride through the city and the poorly paved road to my destination made for a giddy stomach, and the sight of Garphonge Gormona fluttering through the main entry to welcome me made my gorge rise. He had a candelabrum raised with one arm and a repulsively tiny lap dog cradled in the other. The heir's voluminous purple silk robe billowed about in the breeze of the warm night as he approached, sizing me up and speaking baby-jabber to his pet. As he drew near, I was overwhelmed by powerful wafts of the lavender secretions with which he dressed his trim goatee and curiously styled hair. We faced each other, and he dipped to gently put the dog down, then popped up, smiling softly and tilting his head back and forth, waiting and silent. To make a strong impression—and send a message—I shook his dainty and moist hand, every finger of which bore an ostentatious ring, with manly vigor. Apparently, he was taken with me. My hand still in his grasp, he turned and gently tugged me through the door of the mansion. The grand hall was alight with hundreds of candles, as was every room radiating from it. Pulling me along, he led me into the drawing room to sit. The once-stately space was packed with huge bouquets of fragrant flowers. What with the mixture of scents, the warm room, and the endless monologue of my affected host, I felt disoriented and perspired heavily. “Excuse me, but I need to freshen up,” I blurted, instantly halting the epic narrative my host was intently relating. “But of course,” he whispered in sympathy, putting a hand on my knee. “How rude of me to go on so.” He summoned a butler, who led me to a privy. I slipped off my jacket and sat, taking deep breaths until steady, taking stock. I was not in control of the situation. I was not in control of myself. I must take the lead and guide the lamb to the butcher. Then I remembered and retrieved from the hidden pocket of my jacket a yellow packet. I took several pinches of the powdery contents in each nostril, and felt better in an instant. And then two more pinches. Returning to my host, I thanked him, and took the opportunity to present him with one of the gifts I brought along, at DeFleur’s insistence: a bottle of a very rare port—one of a lot of three—that DeFleur purchased at an auction many years ago, and intended to auction at a later date. The resolution of the gallery’s current financial situation depended on the success of my visit, and the port was the perfect token. Garphonge had a known passion for fine ports, spending lavishly on exceptional vintages bottled by defunct producers. He claimed that from the age of fourteen, he took no other liquid but port. I had also heard that his dedication to port was second only to his fondness for hairless boys with moles. Garphonge was delighted by the gift! Opening the bottle with reverence, he poured and we imbibed, the port proving potent and delicious. The moment seemed right to sample the gummy and dark ball, the second item of my purchase from the *chinee* apothecary. He rolled his eyes when he saw it. "*How* did you *know*?" he gushed, giving me a wink. Calling for his major domo, he dismissed the staff until noon. Sitting uncomfortably close to me, and dipping his finger daintily in the little heap of powder I emptied onto the table in front of us, he whispered: "And now, Mr. Gambon, let us get the matter of those dreary paintings out of the way."

It was a fait accompli once he made it evident he had taken a shine to me . . . oh, the thought! But I worked my magic for all it was worth. Thoroughly inebriated by the end of our negotiation, the fool had difficulty signing his own name. Though he attempted to read through the complicated agreement, I doubt he had any idea of the net amount he would be paid or even to whom he was selling the collection. The papers he squinted at through one eye most likely appeared to be a gray field composed of tiny squiggling glyphs. That is what I saw while flipping through the pages, awaiting his signature, and I was in the same state as he. Frustrated, he at last inked his name and breathed a sigh of relief. He turned to me, softly saying, "And now, Janos, you must uphold your end." Pressed by the catamite, I had relented to partake in certain specific activities as an unwritten addendum to the contract. . . .

By dawn the next day, two powerful houses had fallen, and another—mine—rose, like a phoenix, from the piles of their ashes. DeFleur would be undone by my deceit, for the heir had sold the paintings to *me*, signing the agreements I had printed before departing for Castaphon. There was no argument from the seller, with whom I woke in bed the next morning. His cold, stiff form offered mute testimony to the power of the narcotics he favored, and which I had so thoughtfully provided. Garphonge having no further need of DeFleur's money, I relieved him of the burden. Calling for my carriage, I carefully packed away the collection

and a few other baubles fit to take. One last visit to my stiff host verified that no clues were left behind, but, just for insurance, I moved the candelabra perhaps a little *too* close to the drapery and wood wainscoting. My personal version of the Proof..........................
....
....
....
....
....
....
....
....
....
....
....
....
....
....
....
....
....
....
....
....
....
....
....
....
....
....
....
....
....
....
....
....
....
....
....

....
....
....
....
....
....
....
....
....
....
....
....
....
....
....
....
....
....
....

So many details! My head was swimming with all the trivial particulars that needed attention and by the time the problems were resolved, the first Proof was upon us! The weeping families were allowed a last visit; how sad it must have been for them, a horrifying experience. The diet of maggots was not nearly as nutritious for the contestants as the contestants would soon be to the maggots! Also horrifying was the fact that the champions were bound to six-meter wooden stakes, and swaddled and bundled about with strips of burlap dipped in tallow, and rare oils, and flammable solvents, and lastly, several thick coats of creosote, ensuring fast adherence of the chosen to their poles. The families bade farewell and were led to the escarpment—my current and final locus—and given seats of honor.

Clearing my throat loudly for attention, I addressed the town populace with a somber little speech and in closing offered the hope that once again peace would settle on the town, and we could all resume a normal existence. The throng was silent and respectful, but the collective tension was palpable. I moved to the box housing the switch that, when thrown, would send a spark through the wires and ignite the partisans on the cliff. The complicated ignition machine was cobbled together by the town tinker, Magbo, for the safe firing of celebratory flares and whiz-bangs fashioned by the *chinee* apothecary for the town's tercentenary celebration. Soon the machine's numerous parts were set and ready. At Posthumo's nod, I threw the switch, and the two cocoons simultaneously exploded into flames with a loud POP, flaring high and bright under the full moon that floated overhead. Such a sight! I doubt the contestants survived very long in the consuming infernos, but nothing could be heard over the roar of the flames. The intense brilliance of the conflagrations forced me to avert my eyes several times, but Posthumo's unblinking scrutiny of the event made me wonder if the hermit was actually blind, making his way by some unknown extra sense.

Those closest reported the fires were extremely hot. From my vantage point, they burned with a white, wavering incandescence, almost *molten*, entirely consuming the contestants and the stakes within five minutes' time, at which point the stakes burned through. Pokolo's spectacular diagonal fall evoked a collective gasp from the assembly, quickly repeated when the stake holding Lofus toppled crosswise over his rival's remains, forming a scorching and broken X. The crossed heaps continued to flare and crackle, and the crowd watched in silent horror and awe, wondering, like myself, which of the champions would be declared the victor. Both burned with near-blinding magnitude, to my eyes. I looked to Posthumo, hoping for a sign, but the hermit's keen gaze did not waver from the event. The crowd, starting to buzz, turned my way for an indication. I shrugged in return.

At last, the ancient recluse stepped forward. Raising a hand for silence, Posthumo proclaimed, with clear voice and authority: "The Great Lights of the Sphere declare this trial a dead heat, both of the chosen being judged unworthy of the trial! The Proof must be repeated to chasten the dark malice which blinds the eyes and withers the souls of this town!" Pulling his threadbare wrap close, Posthumo stalked through the parting throng and disappeared into the dark woods, presumably to his hovel.

The perplexed gathering swirled in slow circles of confusion, mumbling and grousing in small groups for a spell before heading home to warm beds as the embers of the failed contestants cooled.

I thought it crucial that a more empirical method of light measuring be employed; otherwise, all the artists would end up as tinder. After thanking the stragglers for attending the event, I, too, left the site of the atrocity, questioning the hermit's motives and his "spiritual" agenda. Were we of Rawwoody mere pawns in his plan? And to what end? But I now know better—Posthumo's search is a quest for purity and essence; he seeks the brilliant glow of profound inspiration over the dulling murk of mediocrity, his presence and pure heart a requisite of judgment. And so he chose *me*. I suspect that I am the last of the contestants to be so honored.........
....
....
....
....
....
....

....
....
....
....
....
....
....
....
....

Ah, poor DeFleur. On my return from Castaphon, his end of our entire conversation comprised only two words, the first, an impatiently barked "So?" upon my entering the gallery, looking as haggard and upset as possible.

So.

Feigning the distress appropriate in the wake of such a harrowing experience, I stuttered out the facts I preferred to remember: The successful purchase had been completed as planned, and the lengthy agreements signed. I handed over the bag of currency to Garphonge, who called for his head butler, who received the bag from his master with a bow and left the room without a word. Since it was quite late at this point, the heir suggested I spend the night, and gather and wrap the paintings in the morning, when I was fresh. Accepting his offer, I planned to depart at noon the next day.

But, alas, I was awakened early in the morning, choking from smoke, and barely made it out of the inferno alive. The legal documents, the paintings, the cash—all were gone, consumed in the spectacular conflagration of the mansion.

DeFleur stared right through me with narrowed eyes, unconvinced. He knew. His face reddened, the veins in his neck bulging in anger. Taking a crooked step in my direction, DeFleur blurted out, "YOU!" The old cheat's mouth froze on that word, for a second, an eternity, eyes bulging and mouth open and gasping, a truly hideous sight. He toppled to the floor as his lame leg failed, panting as desperately as a beached shark. An unnerving moment, but a perfect one as well, one that eliminated the risk of retribution from *the* master of dastardly deeds. For an hour, I watched DeFleur writhe and gasp—several snifters of his excellent brandy helping to pass the time—before yelling in impatient panic for one of the bin boys to fetch the physician. DeFleur expired that evening. Had he been able to speak, I like to think that his last words to me would be: "Well played, Gambon! Well played!" But I satisfied myself with his secret trove of cash and the most important collection of historical art in private hands.

I handled the modest funeral arrangements and was

impressed by the turnout. Every remaining dealer showed up, of course, hoping to poach a loose client or two. Many of DeFleur's oldest clients attended as well, though most looked as if they would soon be joining their consultant. I even paid homage to DeFleur's discriminating eye and scholarship and kept the encomium very general. It was a bore but expected of me.

Of course, I was subsequently questioned by swarms of jurists, town accountants, and provincial tax authorities regarding the labyrinthine mysteries of DeFleur's record keeping, but my ignorance of these matters was not feigned, as I was never privy to this end of the business. The untangling of DeFleur's arcane ledgers continues to this day, as provincial and Rawwoody tax officials haggle over his estate, essentially consisting of the gallery's inventory, which most likely will be auctioned to pay the considerable tax debts of the business.

Maintaining a quiet life following DeFleur's demise, I at last had the time and resources to concentrate on painting. When the time was right, I contacted a young collector, shy and eccentric, who had expressed interest in the Gormona pictures when DeFleur was testing the waters. I sold him the entire collection, at a bargain price, when he visited to inspect the paintings. No documents accompanied the transfer of ownership and we struck a gentleman's agreement that the paintings were never to be loaned for exhibition, to which he readily agreed, being of a private nature.

In self-imposed solitude, I continued to paint—and to consider my next business move, for I sorely missed the social whirl that was essential to the trade. After considerable reflection, the notion of creating a gallery featuring the work of promising living artists seemed the most attractive option. Many established artists were seeking representation at this time, their galleries crippled or closed, for the flat economy showed few indications of recovery. I envisioned a stable of artists from both sides of the strife, attracting collectors from each group. This was my plan, but such an enterprise was a risk, as evidenced by the number of vacant contemporary galleries forced to close down—referred to as "temporary" galleries by the bitter and now rootless artists previously represented. Embarking on a quiet return to the trade, I nonetheless became the subject of speculation and rumor. After searching for a location to set up my gallery, I decided to move outside the established art district and its tainted history, and leased an empty and spacious street-level space on the west side of Rawwoody, engaging masons and carpenters to alter it to my specifications. I was not alone in my thinking, as two other shop fronts were being readied for similar ventures. On meeting these supportive gamblers, I was struck by their ambition and vision and continued on my plan with confidence.

As my gallery was being readied, I enjoyed a fruitful period of painting, making great leaps in my work: three easel paintings of incomparable unity and solidity, as if sculpture had been flattened onto canvas. These are my masterpieces, which have elevated me to the current position of distinction I now inhabit, and which will illuminate the lives and histories of all who follow my standard..
....
....
....
....
....
....
....
....
....
....

The Tribunal met the morning following the first trial of the Proof. They unanimously agreed that an objective means of judgment for the contests must be found. I volunteered to look into the possibilities. Though not expressly stated by any of the committee members, I sensed a strong undercurrent of unease about the judgment of the dead heat. Posthumo's motives became a brief topic of discussion, but soon sputtered away. So little was known about the ancient mystic and his arcane ways. The meeting proved pointless, in the end raising more questions than answers. When the meeting adjourned, I left with the feeling that things most definitely were not under our control.

While in the area, I took a slight detour to visit the shop of Magbo, the town tinker who had volunteered the ignition machine that simultaneously fired the first two contestants. A clever and well-educated man, quiet and thoughtful and of pleasant demeanor, Magbo spent more time studying the esoteric advancements of the "physical sciences" than he ever would repairing tin pots and keening knives. Buying a bottle of quality nip, if there is such a thing, I headed for his shop. The door was open to the breeze, and there he sat, feet up, reading a book as thick as a paving stone. My soft knock drew his attention. "Cheers," I said, lifting the nip. The tinker—"thinker" is more appropriate, haha—waved me in, pushing a chair my way with a foot. After a cup or two, I told him of the Tribunal's need of a way to accurately measure the brightness of light.

"You mean light from burning artists?" His question had a sarcastic edge.

I nodded. He pointed at a bulky wooden box in a corner, a contraption with a large glass embedded in one side and many hinges. Explaining that once the details of the Proof process spread through town, he was intrigued by the nature of the challenge. He called it a "light gauge." When I asked if it worked, he shrugged. Sheets coated with powdered virgin silver were needed, but beyond his means; but in theory it should work, especially at night. I told him to order, and quickly, whatever was needed, enough to test his light gauge, and for use in the Proof trials, guaranteeing the Tribunal would underwrite his costs. We shook hands on the deal and I left, confident that Magbo's machine would work. One week later, the tinker performed several tests using burning bundled pig carcasses in the presence of the Tribunal. Impressed by the results, Magbo was appointed the official Light Judge as Posthumo accepted the man and his mechanical miracle without the benefit of a demonstration. I had fulfilled my task.................

....
....
....
....
....
....
....
....
....
....
....
....
....
....
....
....
....
....

Shortly after the first Proof, while on a stroll, I happened upon the inseparable duo of Quince Whimper and Birgle Pilferd, business neighbors and co-owners in the fresh venture of the Pilferd-Whimper Salon. Animated and in high spirits, they were celebrating the success of the inaugural exhibition of their gallery—they were quite the Jollies! The duo reported with good cheer and gusto a great surge in the market for their incinerated artist, Lofus. They thanked me profusely for my role in their success. I heard similar murmurs from the remaining Formalist dealers as well—very quiet talks, as you can imagine, the subject not lending itself to

scandalous thought of profit, yet, there it was; we were forging a new market tool with the Proof trials, just as we were forging new aesthetic proofs, the perfect symbiosis, like the sparks that livened the wires to the contestants...
....
....
....
....
....
....

Posthumo was conspicuously absent for much of the ensuing month, but magically appeared when a critical matter of protocol arose. An unaffiliated sculptor, by the name of Selsius of Colarie, had petitioned the Magistrates and the Tribunal to be admitted to the next contest. He was current on the fast, he claimed, and, though politically neutral, argued that he wanted to challenge the established schools of aesthetic thought with his personal vision. The Tribunal censured the actions, but the city Magistrates and Court, to whom the verdict was appealed, agreed to a hearing. Posthumo appeared at the meeting, unbidden, and solemnly listened to the deranged logic and incoherent rants of Selsius, which confounded the officials and ultimately led to legal squabbling among the court officers.

Posthumo cut the arguments short. Struggling to his feet, he faced the officials, declaring: "This man is worthy to participate in the trials."

The court watched in stunned silence as the hermit hooked his emaciated arm around the shoulders of Selsius and led him away into the fold of the anointed and soon to burn. The convened jurists ratified the artist's petition after the fact. All I knew of the new contestant—aside from his secretive skulking in the shadows as he appropriated from refuse containers of various merchants—was that he had clobbered down Godulfus, taking great offense at one of the sculptor's obscene rants about religion. My contacts informed me Selsius had a large family who had suffered with his individual fanaticism for many years. Living in squalid poverty and scorned by their neighbors, the clan was mortified by the strange and often violent actions of the man. The frequent incarcerations of Selsius were incurred in his personal quest for perfection that was beyond any mortal's understanding.

I decided to pay the family a visit—not as the head of the Tribunal, but out of my curiosity about the artist's work. I arrived in a wagon filled with groceries. The rambling, ramshackle building that housed the brood was alive with shrieks of nervous despair, and the dirt yard teemed with half-naked brats engaged in a battle of sticks and stones. The war stopped when I climbed off the wagon and asked for their mother. What a sight she was! I've never seen a woman so beaten down by life—there was absolutely no light in her eyes. I introduced myself, explaining I had come to help them and was interested in seeing the work of Selsius. She ushered me into the squalor of the house, and the crowd of noisy urchins followed, fighting over the contents of the baskets and sacks I had brought along. She dropped to her knees crying and thanking me for the gift. I was thoroughly embarrassed by the scene and helped her up, stuttering once again my interest in her husband's work. I followed her through the labyrinth of rooms to the studio.

The visionary was quite prolific; the large room and its walls were filled with the manic energy that defined her mate. I was drawn immediately to a sizeable temple that dominated the center of the room. A closer look revealed it was made entirely from lint. His wife told me Selsius collected the combings from tailors who saved it for him and its construction took years to complete. The work possessed a naïve quality, but also one of great determination and necessity. Under the right conditions, and if marketed properly, it could be sold, and better yet, collected. Feeling certain about this point, I quickly made myself a smart deal for the entire artistic estate of her husband. It was more money than she could imagine, and she wept throughout the remainder of my visit, which hastened my departure.

By the time of the diet of worms, the excitement in town was building again—and this time, with the third contestant, a new faction appeared in the crowd, championing the underdog Selsius. The Proof proceedings seemed to be moving away from the political sphere to the sphere of personality, and Selsius was well represented by his own motley throng. There was a much merrier mood about this one; handicappers were doing good business, taking the bets—the two-to-one favorite being Galney Pinch. I, of course, had my own favorite...
....
....
....
....
....
....

I had a novel idea around this time about showing and marketing my own art, since the attrition rate of artists was on the rise, and I thought there might be several niches my work could fill. I had shown no one my work for years, and I would have been surprised if anyone had remembered that I was a painter at all, though I had been scrupulously putting in my time at the easel. I hired a quite comely, indigent student, Belana, as an assistant-her first task was to make the rounds of the dealers pretending my pictures to be her own creation. At best, my work was rejected without comment. Poor girl—at my insistence, she reported in detail the results of her foray, and the sweet dear tried to spare my pride from the lack of interest in my paintings. But I could not help pressing her for all the details of her meetings. The unkindest cut came from that fool Gromanzer Rezaw, who shook his head with the remark that "such paintings are a waste of good canvas." She did relate that she was stopped in the square by a queer old man, who asked if he could see, and she showed him the work, which he studied ever so long.

He then closed his eyes, and with face tilted skyward, said, "Thank you!" and to my girl he said, "Thank you for the look into such a soul . . ."

I asked her who this man was, but she had never seen him before, having only recently arrived, and I guessed

that he was one from the endless stream of vagrants, victims of the ruined economy, who passed through town for handouts before continuing their journey to oblivion.....
....
....
....
....
....
....
....
....
....
....
....
....
....
....
....
....

The event went flawlessly. Selsius was the winner, as revealed by Magbo's machine. To the naked eye, it looked close, but there was no disagreement from any quarter, including Posthumo's. I congratulated the family of Selsius (and myself) on the victory. The crowd indulged in an all-night revel following the contest, and their exhilaration was so high that I decided to put on a bigger and better show next time, as the bloody rivalry between the art factions was yet to be settled.

The two weeks following Selsius's triumphant burn were the best of my entire life. I never have felt so energetic, positive, and decisive. I harped on the tradesmen to finish my gallery, for the opening would be the first exhibition of works by Selsius. There was great curiosity about the reclusive sculptor, who seemingly appeared from thin air to best the champions of the established schools of aesthetic thinking. The elevation of Selsius provided Rawwoody with an unforeseen benefit, for he became the one subject on which both of the radical factions could agree. Soon the two sides were speaking again, united against a common enemy whose work they considered intellectually vacuous, poorly executed, and, in general, awkwardly naïve. However, few, if any, of the orators had seen a single work by the shy Selsius. I was confident that my gallery's inaugural exhibition of his works would be crammed with the curious and the jealous, along with the usual crowd.

The Tribunal convened two weeks before the next full moon. I intended to acknowledge my ownership of Selsius's artistic estate, which I purchased simply out of a deeply felt concern for the family's well-being, and so on and so forth. I was rather nervous about this issue, as my actions could possibly be interpreted as a conflict of interest. I also wished to propose larger Proofings, perhaps six artists at once, but decided to raise the issue at a later date, having plenty to explain away today.

The first item on the agenda, however, was the lottery to determine the participants of the upcoming Proof trial. I glanced around as the ballots were being collected from both groups of solemn partisans. Posthumo discreetly stood in a corner, preoccupied, his brow furrowed in thought. He suddenly glanced up and we locked eyes. A smile broke across his wrinkled face, his head nodding, as if in understanding, and the hermit clapped his hands for attention. All activity ceased, and every eye focused on the mystic.

Spreading his arms wide, he faced the court. "There is but one who must face the Proof!" he proclaimed in a clear voice. The hermit slowly turned until his outstretched hand pointed directly at me and stopped. "It is only he who must face the final trial of fire," he said solemnly.

I have never been so exhilarated as at that moment.
....
....
....
....
....
....
....
....

....
....
....
....
....
....
....
....
....
....
....
....
....
....
....
....
....
....
....
....
....

It occurs to me that there are many similarities between Posthumo and DeFleur, though the styles of expression are polar opposites—Posthumo being quietly insistent, DeFleur obnoxiously repetitive and loudly nasty. But both would not leave any query to go unanswered, and would niggle and badger and tease till satisfied with a response they sensed as the truth. I did not get a wink of sleep in the weeks of my fast and paltry diet of worms—I do not know how Posthumo stayed clear and alert the whole time, he being so aged and seemingly fragile, but he was there to ensure I was conscious every moment of the regimen of enforced training for eternal life and fame.

Stripped naked immediately upon arriving at the hermit's hut, he gave me a choice of flails—one of leather, the other of felt. I chose the felt, half-heartedly flinging it over my shoulder while answering his questions as to my purity of intent, and have I ever cheated someone, and have I ever murdered for gain, or had I ever caused the death of another by self-serving actions, and so on and on and on . . . to all of which I expressed innocence and the purity of intention which guided all of my actions. He would shake his head sadly and start his interrogation again, from a different angle, but I do not think he was aware of my being an art dealer, and immune to any one version of the truth, there being many, and many more that were dormant for the time being. But he never gave any indication of frustration at my answers, and kept preaching purity and essence and charity. . . .

Once, we locked eyes and he stared deep and long, till I blinked; nodding his head, he said: "Yes, you will burn the brightest, you will blind the sighted, but you will never sight the blind." What that meant, I have no idea, but was relieved when he looked away. Then . . . What, what is that? Oh no! No! Yes!

They are coming! I hear voices! And the moon—it is nearly overhead—my time of apotheosis has come! Oh! I can hardly breathe! . . . They are coming . . . they are coming . . . they are coming . . .

They were coming. The town's populace tramped in single file along the crude trail that led up to the knoll, their torches held high to illuminate the uneven path. In festive spirits, their exuberant chattering was a constant buzz. Occasional laughter at the vulgar jokes of their neighbors punctuated the babble of their good-natured hysteria as the rabble slowly made its way to the point of destination, a long zigzag of points of light threading through the woods.

At the head of the line were the vendors, and the first to arrive was the pie man, who took up a prime position at the base of the hillock, and bustled about preparing his portable shop, haranguing his help to hurry and doling out an occasional cuff. Nearby, the taverner was tapping two hogsheads of ale, for there was nothing like a good swig to help wash down the pies. A juggler roamed through the gathering crowd, his wit causing currents of laughter in his wake. The meadow at the foot of the knoll was soon teeming with the townsfolk, but still they filed in from the woods to observe the proceedings, this final exhibition of its kind.

The artists were the last to arrive. The Romantics came first, the Formalists following, the groups separated by the solemn and tottering Posthumo assisted by a boy.

Goularti, the Romantic, guided the lad who had just that evening arrived to take up his apprenticeship, and who had passed this way only hours before. The boy looked apprehensive, but his kind master put an arm about his shoulders and pushed through the crowd to the front. As he waited shivering in the cold, he heard a little girl nearby ask why the man on the stick had blood all over his face, and she said "Oh" when her mother answered, "The pest-birds."

The apprentice was told what to expect, but the horror of the event was beyond his ken, and he, like the little girl, simply answered, "Oh." The crowd had quieted. Tired but attentive, and freezing in the cold, he watched an ancient man with long thin hair and a beard to match, wearing but a sere blanket that flapped in the breeze to reveal his nakedness, slowly ascend the slope of the knoll with the aid of a boy. From the other side of the incline, a man unspooled two cables as he walked backward up to the summit, and then to the tall stake that held the bundled man. Placing the wires just so, he retreated from the knoll to take his place behind a cumbersome wooden box, waiting with the rest.

Finally attaining the crest, the ancient one turned to face the throng below. In a surprisingly clear and authoritative voice, he announced: "My time here will soon be finished, and I will be gone before the embers die. . . . There shall be no need for further trials of Proof hereafter, as the infection will be cleansed and the stars once again will smile on you. But remember forever, and pass down the word of the dire and blasphemous events that led to these purifications. . . . Use your special talents to strive against the great void, which threatens to engulf us all. . . . Heed this event with consideration and care, for its occurrence can restore the clarity of vision and purity of purpose that was fouled by the criminal and selfish vanity of those who provoked its occasion."

Posthumo paused. His eyes slowly closed while his free arm lifted apace, pointing a crooked and trembling finger skyward. The eyes of every man, woman, and child hypnotically followed the gesture to behold the full moon directly overhead, in line with the staked contestant and the aged hermit.

"The celestial eye bears witness to these proceedings, as shall you. Use your efforts, and your insight, to define the truth. . . . Truth—it is such a simple thing, often overlooked and easily forgotten. Thus, you must remember."

The silence following Posthumo's speech was profound, but through it all, the apprentice could hear the faint sobbing of the man on the stake.

The old man made a motion to those below who were nearest to him and, without thinking, the apprentice scrambled up the side. Posthumo grabbed his arm and squeezed, offering a smile. Flanked by his own assistant and the apprentice, they gingerly guided the frail ancient off the crest of the hill and onto level ground. The old man said nothing, but did not let loose his grip on the boy's arm. Posthumo peered to the left, nodding to the man who had set and fixed the cables and who was waiting for the sign. He nodded in assent and threw a lever on the side of his wooden contraption.

A quick pop was followed by the nearly deafening roar as the bundle atop the stake exploded into brilliant flame. The crowd gasped as one, the collective "Ohhh!" followed by rapt silence, as the intensity of the flames grew brighter and brighter still, so blindingly radiant that the apprentice shut his eyes. Still, the radiance leaked through his eyelids as the most intense red imaginable, one that he knew could never be duplicated with pigment. The apprentice was oblivious to the cold and his shivers until the hermit loosed his grip and motioned the lad up the knoll with a quirk of his head. Obediently, the boy scrambled to the top, edging slowly toward the raging flames to warm himself, then closer still. Although the blaze burned with blinding brilliance, it offered little heat.